# The Red Scarf

### Eileen F. Drilling

and

### Judith A. Rothfork

*This is a work of fiction. While names of actual historical figures and events have been included, all other names, characters, places and incidents are used fictitiously. Any resemblance to actual persons, living or dead, are entirely coincidental.*

First Edition

Cover design by Judith A. Rothfork
Copyright 2004

Judeen Publishing

*Printed in the United States of America*

ISBN 0-9762152-0-9

1. Great Depression    2. World War II    3. Grief
4. Forgiveness    5. Religious Tolerance    6. Historical Fiction

*We dedicate this book to*

*Tom and other peacemakers*

*all over the world*

# Acknowledgements

We would like to thank the reference personnel
at the Rum River Branch of the Anoka County
Library for their invaluable assistance.  Also we
thank our dear friends,  Dolores Martinson and
Hope Stewart for providing added resources
regarding the Great Depression and World War II.


Special thanks to our loyal friend, Paula Kaempffer,
who helped with her computer skills.

# The Red Scarf

Eileen F. Drilling

and

Judith A. Rothfork

# CHAPTER 1

## *The Mortgage - September, 1941*

Ruthie woke up at six o'clock. Her right ankle felt numb where her sister Margie's foot had rested on it during the night. Something tight in Ruthie's stomach kept her curled up like a spring. She heard her sister snore in small spurts. Carefully she uncurled herself, then tiptoed downstairs to get some water.

When she turned at the bottom of the wooden stairs, she saw a light in the kitchen. Mother stood by the sink looking out the back window. Ruthie crept toward the door ready to shout, "Boo!" She stopped abruptly when she saw her mother wipe her eyes with the edge of her pink apron. She was crying. A lump formed in Ruthie's throat and she silently backed out of the kitchen.

Something creaked in the dining room. From a slit of light coming from the kitchen, she saw her brother, Herman, peeking into a buffet drawer where Dad kept the mortgage money. For six o'clock on a Sunday morning in the Schmit house, there seemed to be a lot going on.

Herman quickly shut the drawer and jerked back when he saw her. "What are you doing up so early?" he scowled, embarrassed at being discovered.

"Mom is crying in the kitchen," Ruthie's voice cracked. She was close to tears of her own.

"Crying?" Herman settled his feelings by gathering facts. "Let's see, Aunt Bea will come to collect the mortgage money after church today. We're poor. That's why Mom is crying."

When he realized Ruthie's sadness, he continued, hoping to soothe her, "Our country is in a depression. That means just about everybody else is poor, too, but President Roosevelt is working on it. Pretty soon everyone will have jobs. We're lucky Dad works for the county highway department."

Ruthie admired her twelve year old brother, who seemed to understand things faster and with more detail than herself but that didn't help her feel any better about seeing her mother cry. She went back upstairs to get dressed for church. Margie stood by the mirror, pinning a lavender paper flower on the purple taffeta dress she had made in Home Economics class for the Mother-Daughter Banquet last year.

"Margie, Mother is crying in the kitchen."

"Aunt Bea is coming today. It's the mortgage. Mom will be all right. Don't worry about it," Margie responded.

"Aunt Bea, Aunt Bea, Aunt Bea," Ruthie mumbled. "That's why my stomach is all tight. I hate her." Ruthie pulled her yellow cotton dress roughly from the hanger in the closet. "We are poor. We have to share the closet, the bedroom and even the bed. And it's all because of Aunt Bea. It's not fair. I bet the kids on the north side of town each have their own bedroom." Still mumbling she dressed for church.

Ruthie usually liked Sundays because her mother put chocolate in the oatmeal and served it on dinner plates, so Ruthie and Herman could make rivers and lakes with milk by pushing the oatmeal into hills and valleys. Margie, a junior in high school, thought the oatmeal plate was babyish.

Although the two girls shared their dislike of Aunt Bea, they often argued. Margie told her mother, "It's not fair to have a ten year old sister share my bedroom."

"Well, it's not fair for me either," Ruthie complained.

To Ruthie it seemed like Margie spent hours before their bedroom mirror combing her natural wavy blonde hair, while she had to use the bathroom mirror to get ready for school. Margie used more closet space and got the extra dresser drawer. Even her typewriter and desk stood on Ruthie's side of the room.

But on Sundays Margie was usually in a good mood because the Schmits did things together that were fun. Sometimes they'd go to Uncle Jim's farm. Forgetting to be lady-like, Margie would race to the windmill and climb to the top, even though her hands turned black from the years of dust collected on the rungs, and the golden strands of her carefully combed hair became tousled by the wind. Being the oldest, she took it upon herself to supervise everyone's turn dunking in the horse tank filled with cold water. Sometimes, Ruthie liked it when Margie took control of things. It felt safe. At other times, she got angry at her bossiness.

Usually Ruthie led the hunt for the baby kittens in the barn. Herman opened the trap door in the hay mow for everyone to jump from the top floor into a pile of hay on the first floor. Once when her best friend, Billy, was along, he slipped off the sweet smelling hay right into a pile of manure. Cow dung stained his shirt and pants. The children laughed as Billy rushed to the horse tank to clean it off and then enjoyed a second dunk before Uncle Jim saw him and put a halt to the fun.

Ruthie liked Sunday nights the best. The parlor became a dance floor. Mrs. Schmit entertained her family, playing honky-tonk music on the piano. Mr. Schmit strummed along on the banjo he had ordered from the Sears Roebuck catalogue for twelve dollars. By studying the enclosed instructions, he had taught himself to play it. Margie taught Ruthie and Herman dance steps and they all sang and danced together. Tonight would be even more fun with Aunt Bea's visit over. She could forget her aunt and the mortgage for four more weeks.

"Ruthie, you're daydreaming. Come on. I smell breakfast."

When Ruthie entered the kitchen the second time that morning, she studied her mother's face. Her spirit lightened as if a heavy blanket had dropped from her shoulders. The tight knot in her stomach disappeared when she saw her mother smile. Mrs. Schmit poured the chocolate oatmeal on two plates. Ruthie poured the morning's fresh goat milk on the steaming cereal and plunged in her spoon like a bulldozer. Soon she was lost in creating a world of rivers, lakes and dams.

After breakfast, Mother gave the all too familiar reminder, "Girls, remember to wear the hats that Aunt Bea gave you, since we'll be seeing her today."

Margie looked at Ruthie and rolled her eyes with disgust.

# CHAPTER 2

*Aunt Bea and Billy*


At quarter to eight, Mr. Schmit pulled the tan car from the garage. Ruthie exclaimed, "Doesn't it look elegant? I'm glad Dad's boss gave us his second hand Whippet. Now we don't have to walk to church."

"No, Dad's boss didn't *give* the car to us," Herman explained. "Dad has to pay him some money each month. That's why it's harder to pay the mortgage this time." Then he leaned closer to Ruthie's ear and whispered, "That's probably why Mom was crying this morning."

Later in church, Ruthie spotted Aunt Bea coming down the aisle. Her tall angular body remained straight as a steel pole when her knee touched the floor in a genuflection. She cut a striking contrast to Billy's family wedged in the same front pew by St. Joseph's statue. Relieved, Ruthie noticed cousin Arnold wasn't with Aunt Bea.

Nudging Herman, she whispered, "Look, she has an ugly gray hat." Aunt Bea's hats seemed to indicate her moods. Today she would be like the gray sky, businesslike and a world away from the poverty of the Schmits and the other common homes in Billy's and Ruthie's neighborhood.

Margie glared at her siblings and put her finger to her lips, "Shhh!"

Ruthie saw Billy, dressed in a black cassock and white surplus, waiting to ring the bell to announce the beginning of Mass. She liked it when he served the Mass as an altar boy. Not only was he her best friend, he was her third cousin and seemed like part of the family. His parents rented a house two blocks away but he practically lived at Ruthie's.

Margie often said, "Ruthie, you're too old to have a boy for your best friend, unless he is your boyfriend."

But Ruthie defended herself, "His mother is our second cousin. We're just plain friends. We go with Herman to the city dump to look for things, or to watch Herman shoot rats with his BB gun. Would we do that if he was my boyfriend?"

Billy was a giggler. She hoped he wouldn't giggle in front of Aunt Bea who was even stricter than Father Weaver now beginning Mass. Though she tried to get down to the business of praying, she kept an eye on Billy. She held her breath during the quiet times, fearing he'd break out into giggles.

After the service, the tightness in Ruthie's stomach returned when she sighted Aunt Bea and Cousin Arnold waiting for them at the bottom of the church steps. Arnold wore a red scarf which he kept flipping over the shoulder of his brown plaid sports coat.

"He's just showing off his fall outfit," Margie muttered.

Arnold smirked contentedly as he tapped ashes off his cigarette. Billows of smoke surged from his mouth, reminding Ruthie of a snorting dragon. A senior in high school, he felt it his privilege to stand in the back of church during services so he could occasionally slip out for a smoke.

By now Billy had sidled over to the Schmit family. Covering one side of his mouth with his hand, he leaned toward Ruthie and whispered, "Arnold probably snuck out during the sermon to smoke a cigarette and missed all that stuff Father Weaver said about being humble."

Ruthie smiled, then noticed some red dots on Billy's face and arms. She wondered if something was wrong but there was no time to ask him. Unaware of his red dots, Billy smirked back at Arnold, then walked past him so closely he brushed the cigarette from his hand.

"Oops" he said and ran to join his own family, who had begun their hike home.

Aunt Bea straightened her black dress. Ruthie noticed that her beige cotton stockings wrinkled around her ankles. Her lips were thin and straight like a short horizontal line between her nose and chin. Dad gave her two five dollar bills and then they shook hands like business partners.

"Bea, you and Arnold must stop over for a piece of apple pie before you go home," Mother invited.

"Yes, thank you. It sounds delicious,"

The relatives spent an hour at the house. It seemed like forever to Ruthie.

"Why do we have to feed the enemy?" Margie mumbled under her breath as she helped Mother with the dishes after they left.

"She's not the enemy," Mother said. "We owe her the money. And I don't want to hear you talking about your aunt that way anymore."

"Well, Arnold sniffed and snooped in all our cupboards. He doesn't own our house," Margie retorted. "He didn't even take this." She stooped to pick up the red scarf from under the table. "I'm going to keep it."

Mother frowned and shook her head, no.

Coveting the scarf, Ruthie tried to distract her mother, "Why don't they just forget about the mortgage? They're relatives. Relatives should give you money and things if you are poor and they are rich."

Herman kept quiet. Mother sighed. Dad began a familiar speech. "I know Bea is my sister and they do have money, but this is a business deal. We shall never take charity from anyone or go on welfare."

Margie mouthed his words silently, sighing loudly to let everyone know she had heard this sermon a hundred times before. Mother glared at her. Ruthie remembered mother at the kitchen sink crying. Taking charity or going on welfare sounded just fine to her right now.

The next day in school her teacher, Sister Paula, announced, "Billy has the measles. He's quarantined. That means he can't come to school for awhile."

Without Billy, her dislike for Aunt Bea felt like a heavy stone in her heart. If he were here, the two would giggle about the dreaded aunt and her nasty son, Arnold.

The whole class seemed to shut down after Sister Paula's announcement, until finally she added, "For art today we can make cards and send them to Billy by mail."

The students clapped.

Immediately Ruthie felt better.

It was a long day. When the dismissal bell finally rang, Ruthie thought again about the red scarf. It would make a great get well gift for Billy. It is so pretty, but of course, they'd have to give it back to Arnold.

# CHAPTER 3
## *Planning A Sale*

Herman and Ruthie sat on the kitchen floor with the radio turned on, waiting for their favorite program, *Fibber McGee and Molly*. Ruthie thought about mortgage Sunday. She said to herself, "I never want to see Mother cry again."

Herman must have been thinking the same thing because he said, "Ruthie, let's have a sale and make some money for the mortgage."

"A candy sale? You mean like the one at school?" Ruthie's mind jumped back to the candy sale last May. The third floor lunch room seemed like a paradise. Red and white crepe paper streamers draped from the center lights to the four corners. Tables were filled with chocolate candy, striped taffy, divinity, fudge and peanut brittle. In one corner of the room, cakes of all sizes, shapes and flavors were in readiness for the cake walk. Another corner was crowded with students hoping to win a prize on the fortune wheel. Each would take a turn spinning a large wheel. Some children crossed their fingers for good luck, closed their eyes tightly and waited breathlessly for the wheel to stop on a prize number. Last year, Herman had won a lamp with a pink ruffle on the bottom of the shade. He gave it to Mom for Christmas.

"Our candy sale won't be as big as the one at school," Herman answered, "but we'll have a show, too. Billy can entertain the audience. He's even funnier than Jack Benny or Fibber McGee."

"I know but Billy has the measles," Ruthie reminded him.

"Aw, that's too bad," Herman groaned. "He'd have everybody laughing."

That was true she thought. For example, Billy had a good singing voice  but he made his voice go up and down in the wrong places during music class. Once Sister Paula asked him if he had a sore throat and told him to get a drink of water.  As he walked out, he winked at Ruthie and covered his giggle with a cough.

Sometimes he giggled accidently, too, like  the day the class took a test.  The room was hushed and Billy started to giggle.  When he couldn't hold his laughter any longer, he broke out into a sputter like the noise of water coming from an unused faucet. Ruthie started laughing.  She tried to stifle it by putting her hand over her mouth. Finally, the whole class snorted and choked as they tried not to laugh.

Sister Paula seemed upset because she walked right out of the classroom.  At least everyone thought she was angry until Lenny, a seventh grader, reported to the boys at recess what he saw when coming back from the lavatory. "Hey, guys, what was so funny in class this afternoon?  I saw Sister Paula laughing hilariously in the hallway. When she saw me, she stuffed a handkerchief in her mouth.  I suppose she didn't want me to hear her."

Billy didn't laugh about everything.  There were things that bothered him, too. He stumbled over words when he read. Once he said "fart her" instead of "farther." The class thought he was joking and howled. Billy got red in the face and clamped his mouth tight shut. Ruthie knew he wasn't joking. Another time he lost a quarter his mother had given him to buy bread and milk after school. He searched the floor and took everything out of his desk. Ruthie saw his lips quiver and thought he was about to cry. He got up quickly, grabbed his stubby pencil with the eraser bitten off and went to the cloakroom doorway to sharpen it. Turning her head slightly, Ruthie saw Billy wipe his eyes with his elbow-patched blue shirt.

Even though she had scraped dishes every night for five weeks to earn money for the candy sale, Ruthie reached into her own desk, right below the ink well. She took out a white handkerchief. Carefully she untied the knot that held her precious quarter. Should she give it to Billy? She knew his family was poorer than hers. Pretending to tie her shoe, she slipped the money behind the wrought iron leg of Billy's desk. When he returned he discovered it. Ruthie smiled as she heard a surprised gasp. She guessed he never knew it was her quarter.

"We can sing *Whispering Hope* in two parts like last year, when Sister Paula had us go into all eight classrooms," Herman said, nudging her thoughts back to the present.

"But we're not going to stand on chairs. I was so embarrassed when we had to do that, so the kids in the back could see us." Then she added wistfully, "I wish I was a natural entertainer like Billy."

Margie came into the kitchen to listen to the radio program. She overheard the planning. "If you really want to make money, work at a grocery store like I do. I get a dollar every Saturday night," she bragged. "It's a lot of fun wrapping butter, cutting sandwich meat and running all over the store collecting items on customers' lists. But you're both too young. Let Mom and Dad figure out the mortgage."

Ruthie's spirits flattened like a balloon losing air. She knew that Margie excelled in her business subjects in high school. When Margie talked on the phone, she made little squiggles on notepaper and called it shorthand. It looked like a secret code to Ruthie. After Herman found an old typewriter at the city dump and cleaned it up for Margie, she demonstrated how fast she could type. Ruthie figured Margie was right.

Disappointed, Ruthie said, "Herman, maybe we shouldn't have a sale."

"No, let's do it," Herman insisted.

Margie said, "Shh, it's on. Listen."

All three children laughed when they heard Fibber open the closet door. *Bang! Bang! Crash!* It sounded like everything stuffed into his closet fell out. Ruthie loved listening to *Fibber McGee and Molly.*

Herman and Ruthie stayed in the kitchen to continue plans for the sale. Margie went to bed early because she had to work from eight o'clock in the morning until nine at night the next day.

Saturday, after working eight and a half hours, Margie came home at four thirty. She hollered at the cat when it threw up a fur ball, "No wonder Aunt Bea got rid of you, you dumb old cat." Then she disappeared upstairs. She didn't eat supper with the family. Ruthie knew that after working so hard each Saturday, Margie gave her parents half the money she had earned to help pay the mortgage.

Ruthie picked up the cat and stroked it gently, "Cinder, it's not your fault." Even though she and Margie complained about Aunt Bea often, she knew that her aunt was not to be blamed for Cinder's mishap.

After the dishes were finished, Ruthie went upstairs to their bedroom to get her church envelope for Sunday's collection. The door was shut but she went in anyway.

Margie said sullenly, "You're so rude. Knock next time."

Her eyes were red. She had been crying. She sat on the bed with her feet in a basin of water. They stung from standing in the store all day and she had to go back to work for three more hours. Her job didn't seem much fun to Ruthie but she didn't tell her so.

# CHAPTER 4
## *The Sale*

Herman laid out the plan. "Let's buy a bunch of candy bars at the Newton Locker  and sell them for a nickel a piece."

"But what about the money?" Ruthie asked.  "We have only two cents between us."

Faced with the reality of their financial situation, Herman didn't give up.  Herman, the practical, became Herman, the genius.  After school they bought a package of spearmint gum for a penny at the grocery store where Margie worked.  Each chewed two and a half pieces of gum.  Herman found two long sticks.  He pulled the wad of gum out of his mouth and stuck it firmly onto the end of one stick.  Then he handed Ruthie the second stick.

"I still have flavor in mine," Ruthie complained as she reluctantly put her wad of gum onto her stick.  "Oh, well, the mortgage is more important."

The two charged down  the street toward the gutter in front of the jewelry store.  Herman's eyes grew big as silver dollars when he fished out a quarter from the murky mess under the gutter grate.  Grinning, he pried it from the wad of gum on the bottom of his stick and shined it with his sleeve.  Ruthie discovered a dime by the curb in front of the ice cream shop.  When she stooped to pick it up, a gust of wind blew an ice cream bar stick against her leg.

"It's a miracle!" she shouted, when she noticed a big *FREE* printed near the top of the stick. "Let's get our free ice cream bar."

They ran into the shop. Mr. Goldstein smiled when he saw the delight on each face as he handed them the free bar.

"Thanks, Mr. Goldstein," they said as they left the shop to continue their search. Herman gobbled the top half, then handed it to Ruthie. She slowly licked the ice cream from the bottom half.

"Look! There's a nickel by the curb," squealed Ruthie as she swooped it up.

"We've got forty cents. Mmm, that would get us sixteen candy bars if we can buy two for five cents," Herman calculated in his head.

"Newton Locker, here we come," Ruthie yelled as they ran down the street.

Back home, Herman dumped the candy onto the kitchen table.

"What's this?" asked Mother. "That's a lot of candy. Where did you get that much money?"

"Oh, Mom, we're going to have a candy sale," Ruthie exclaimed.

"And we found the money on the street." Herman explained the entire money hunt to mother, who was now enjoying her children's adventure.

"Do you want to use the back part of the garage? You'll have to clean it up after Nanny." The Schmit's goat, Nanny, which Mother milked everyday to provide the family with sweet milk, lived in the back section of the garage. A plywood wall separated Nanny's home from the front, which was a regular car garage for the Whippet.

"Thanks, Mom," they both shouted.

The next day after school, Herman tied the goat to the plum tree next to the garage. Ruthie took hay from the loft and placed it by her. After Herman and Ruthie swept the floor, Mother suggested that they wash the whole room with soap and water. It took the rest of the afternoon.

"I'm tired." Herman plopped down. Nanny chomped on plums and sticks.

"Me, too," sighed Ruthie as she sat down and gently scratched Nanny's ear.

At supper they told Dad and Margie about the candy sale. Margie got involved and made a giant sign that could be read from the street corner.

### *BIG SHOW*

### *&*

### *CANDY SALE TODAY*

### *3:30 P.M.*

The next day Ruthie and Herman got up an hour early to get ready for the sale. They propped the sign on a wooden crate on the front lawn. Then they ran into the garage. Ruthie meticulously placed the candy bars on a card table Mother said they could use. Herman set up the four card table chairs and four wooden chairs from the kitchen.

Mother came into the garage and said, "I made a pan of fudge last night when everyone went to bed. You can sell it at the candy sale this afternoon."

"WOW! I never smelled it," Herman exclaimed. "If I did, I'd have come down to lick the pan."

"I sealed in the aroma by putting a towel under the door," Mother laughed. "The fudge is in the cellar, keeping cool until the sale. You two better get going to school."

"Thanks, Mom," Ruthie put her arms around Mother's waist and gave her a squeeze.

On the way, they passed Billy's house. He was hanging out of a second story window, shouting and waving to all of the kids going by.

"Hey, Billy, we're having a show and candy sale after school today. Wish you could come," Herman shouted.

"I'll save some of Mom's fudge for you," Ruthie added.

After classes, the children hurried home. When they got there, a lady from across the street was sitting in a chair, holding her baby. The neighborhood children were starting to arrive. Ruthie was aghast to see Billy sitting on Mother's milking stool in the back corner. He giggled when he saw Ruthie's surprise.

"Billy, you're still in quarantine, what are you doing here?"

"Tomorrow is my last day. What difference does a few hours make?"

Ruthie saw the woman with the baby move farther away from Billy and sit next to the door. When all of the seats were filled, Herman announced that the show was about to begin. He and Ruthie walked to the front, Billy trailing behind them. They sang *Whispering Hope* and Billy joined Ruthie's alto part.

The audience clapped and whistled enthusiastically. "They sound like angels," the lady with the baby said to mother, who had just stepped into the doorway.

Mother asked Billy, "Will you sing *America the Beautiful?*"

Without hesitation he began. His melodic voice filled the back garage. As he sang, Ruthie noticed that all of Billy's red dots had disappeared. When the song was finished, Billy started to walk quietly back to the milking stool but as the audience whistled and cheered, he leaped into the air and started to dance a jig.

"Time for the candy sale!" Herman shouted.

Quickly everyone raced around the candy table. A low voice startled Ruthie, "I'll take three pieces of fudge and four candy bars." It was cousin Arnold.

Right away, Ruthie thought of the red scarf. "Arnold, you left your scarf at our house."

"That old thing, you can keep it. Mother always told me to help out the poor."

Ruthie's eyes shot an angry look at Arnold. "We don't need your help. Who told you about our sale?"

"I make it my business to find out what's going on in your family."

Billy, standing next to her, said, "You're a spy. You should work for the government. Why don't you join the army and get out of here?"

Arnold threw a dollar on the table. Although secretly happy about the scarf, Ruthie glared as Arnold sneered and walked away without waiting for change.

Within ten minutes they sold all of the candy, except for six pieces of fudge which they had saved for Billy and themselves. Ruthie and Herman would not let Arnold's appearance at the sale spoil their enthusiasm. The two new business partners were elated when they counted one dollar and eighty-eight cents profit.

"You two had a huge success," Mother said at supper that night.

Her eyes got big and round when Herman pulled a folded paper sack out of his pocket and handed it to her saying, "This is to help pay the mortgage."

Tears came to Mother's eyes as she smiled and thanked the children. Then she suggested, "Why not give Billy a quarter because he helped sing?"

"Good idea! I'll give it to him when he comes back to school after his quarantine," Ruthie promised. Then she whispered, "Mother, Arnold was at the sale. He told us to keep the scarf."

Mother wasn't smiling anymore. She was thinking about Billy. "He's still in quarantine?" Mother was shocked. She started to say something else but then stopped. "Let them enjoy their efforts," she thought. She got up to put the children's gift into the top buffet drawer.

"How much money did you make on the candy sale?" Margie asked.

"One dollar and eighty-eight cents," Ruthie glowed.

Margie said, "Wow! I'm going to make some extra money, too. Remember that flower kit at Mosie's Five and Ten? I'm going to make silk flowers. Ruthie, do you want to help sell the flowers on the north side of town? That's where the rich people live." Both girls looked at their father. Margie pleaded, "Can we, Dad?"

He lit his pipe and then hesitated, "We know some of those people." After puffing thoughtfully for a while, he finally nodded his approval.

Then Mother spoke, "I'm going to candle eggs at the hatchery during school hours."

Everyone gasped. This time Mr. Schmit snapped, "No!" Their parents had never argued in front of them. Ruthie's eyes darted like search lights from Mother to Father. Mr. Schmit raised his voice slightly, "I've got a job and you're not going to work."

"Starting Monday," mother continued, matching her voice volume to his. Everyone felt the tension and knew she meant it.

"Mortgage Sunday is coming soon," Mrs. Schmit said, looking at her husband. "We don't have the money. And you are the one who always says that we shall never go on welfare."

Father got quiet after that. His eyes glittered darkly as if they had coal bits in each one. His cheeks got pink. But he didn't say, "No," again.

Aunt Bea and the mortgage...Arnold and his humiliating remarks...Mother and Father arguing...Ruthie felt confused. She wanted to be angry but the red scarf was so beautiful.

# CHAPTER 5

## *Silk Flowers*

During the next four evenings the girls made silk flowers out of the kit Margie bought at Mosie's Five and Ten Cent Store. After school on Friday the girls ran home to get the flowers.

"Ruthie, I'm going to put on my jacket. It's chilly out there."

"Me, too."

As they walked confidently over the railroad tracks, up Main Street to the north side of town, Ruthie crunched the brittle October leaves that had fallen on the sidewalk.

The very first house they tackled was a success.

"Are you from the neighborhood?" the lady in the big Tudor house asked. She was eyeing the girls up and down, noticing their worn jackets and scuffed shoes. "I'll take five."

"That will be twenty-five cents, Ma'am," Margie spoke with a businesslike tone.

No one answered the doorbells of the next three houses. Margie's shoulders slumped.

"There's a big house with a light in one of the windows," Ruthie exclaimed, pointing across the street. "Someone's home."

"Shh, stop yelling and stop pointing." Margie hissed in a low tone. "That's where old lady Rose lives."

"Who's Lady Rose?" Ruthie whispered, whipping her pointer finger behind her back as if a turtle had just snapped at it.

"Old lady Rose is Milly's aunt."

"Well, who's Milly?" Ruthie asked. She was irritated because Margie kept talking about people she didn't know.

"Milly is a classmate of mine. You don't know her. She told me that her Aunt Rose bought farms from people who couldn't pay their bills. These farmers sold their land real cheap because they just couldn't make ends meet. The old lady has money, so she bought up twenty-one farms."

"Twenty-one farms!" Ruthie interrupted.

"Yes, twenty-one. Milly says she's a miser. She closes off the second floor in that big house and lives in just two rooms on the first floor. She uses only one light bulb dangling on a cord over the kitchen sink. She goes to bed early to save electricity."

The two turned the corner and started to walk down the next block.

"Why would someone so rich want to save on her electric bill?"

"For heavens' sake, Ruthie, I don't know." Margie continued, "Anyway, Milly's mom used to take cookies, cakes, and Sunday dinners over to the old lady until...." Margie stopped and rearranged the flowers so the two blue ones were opposite each other and surrounded by the pink and lavender blossoms. Holding them out for Ruthie to admire, she said, "Do you like how I put the colors together?"

"Yes, but what happened?" Ruthie urged Margie to continue the unfinished story.

"Well, I just rearranged them so..."

Ruthie sighed, "Just tell me what happened to Milly's family."

"Oh," said Margie, her memory back on track. "Well, one Saturday Milly took eight sugar cookies to her Aunt Rose. The next day Milly's mom took a fried chicken dinner over and, for some reason or other, threw something in the garbage can. When she opened the lid, guess what she saw in the garbage?"

"What?" Ruthie was intrigued.

"All eight cookies were exactly the way she had wrapped them - never touched."

"Why would she do that?" Ruthie gasped at the thought of throwing away perfectly good cookies.

"Don't you see? The old lady was afraid she was going to be poisoned. She thought Milly's family wanted her to die real quick so they could get her money."

"Oh, that Lady Rose must be really afraid and very sad."

"If you ask me, she's a miser and just downright guilty about all those farms she practically stole from the poor. Probably serves her right." Margie punched out the words. She walked faster and faster until Ruthie had to run to keep up.

Ruthie was thinking about another person, their own Aunt Bea. She knew her aunt owned three farms. Did she take those from the poor? Was she a miser, too?

Dusk began sneaking into darkness. The girls sold flowers at the next six houses and then decided to go home. Their proceeds were one dollar, tired feet, hungry tummies, unsettling questions but happiness to contribute to the mortgage fund.

Later that evening Ruthie asked her father, "Dad, is Aunt Bea a miser?"

Her father emitted a belly laugh at the thought of his older sister hoarding and hiding money. Mr. Schmit put down his book, "When I was born your Aunt Bea was already fourteen years old. I remember that when your grandmother milked the cows, Bea played hide-and-go-seek with us so we wouldn't get the cows nervous. She taught us how to ride the calves. She even took us fishing. Bea was fun.

Her first baby died when it was two days old. That was very difficult for her. I know she's a good mother to Arnold."

Ruthie remembered Arnold's behavior at the candy sale. She wondered if someone could be a good mother and still have a boy as nasty as Arnold.

"But what about now? Does she own a lot of farms?" Ruthie asked.

"Aunt Bea and Uncle Don have three farms. Some people would call them rich. They bought a farm when they first got married. When Uncle Don's parents died he inherited a second farm. Before you were born, they bought our farm. But she's not a miser. She's been good to us."

Ruthie silently disagreed.  Dad might think Aunt Bea is nice but he sure doesn't like mother working to help pay off the mortgage.

# CHAPTER 6
## *Trouble*

The day Mother began candling eggs, Herman and Ruthie stopped at the hatchery after school to see how it was done.

"We are here to see Margaret Schmit," Herman told a man sitting at a desk.

"Come with me, I'll show you where she is," the man answered.

They walked to a back room and the man pulled opened a black canvas drape. The room was dark except for five little boxes that looked like bird houses with a flashlight beaming out of each hole. The boxes were attached to a shelf over five work tables.

"Margaret, you've got company," the man announced.

"Oh, thank you." Mother was surprised. "Have you met each other? Mr. Benson, these are my children. Herman and Ruthie, this is Mr. Benson, the owner of the hatchery."

Herman stuck out his hand and Mr. Benson shook it. "Glad to meet you, Herman. You, too, Ruthie." As Ruthie shook his hand she thought, "Mr. Benson seems like a nice boss for mother."

After Mr. Benson left, Mother demonstrated her work by putting an egg up to the lighted hole in the box. "This egg has no specks inside, so I'll put it into this large crate to be sold to the grocer."

Mother picked up another egg. "Oh, oh! See the specks in this egg? I need to put it into this blue bucket on the floor."

At four o'clock the three of them walked home together. Ruthie asked, "There were five of those bird houses but only four workers. Who else works there?"

"Mr. Benson said that after Christmas he'll hire another person. Right now the money is tight. He'll put an ad in the paper, so we'll just have to wait."

After her first day of work, Mother seemed the same as always. Dad just asked, "How did it go, Margaret?"

"Fine," Mother smiled.

Supper was on time, so the whole family, except Margie,thought things were normal.

"We're working so hard and Aunt Bea doesn't have to work at all," she complained as she helped prepare vegetables for the next day.

"We owe the money, so there's nothing to argue about," Dad said, sipping another cup of coffee.

"Margie, I told you I didn't want to hear you talk about Aunt Bea that way," Mother reminded. "I'm tired and I don't want to talk about it anymore. I think I'll go to bed early tonight."

"Mother never went to bed early before. It's all Aunt Bea's fault," Margie grumbled to Ruthie as they went to their own room.

Frequently Margie stayed up longer to study. Ruthie had gotten used to falling asleep with the light on. She dozed off. The rattle of paper woke her. Margie was crouched at the typewriter. When she saw Ruthie sit up, she covered a piece of stationery with her arm. Ruthie recognized the stationery that Margie got as a birthday present from her employer. Ruthie marveled how a machine could print a thin navy blue line that bordered each piece of paper. It was so pretty.

"What are you typing?" Ruthie asked innocently.

"None of your business." The words hit like a stinging slap. Then with contrition she added, "Oh, well, you might as well be in on it. You hate her, too." Margie pulled the rectangular paper from the machine and showed it to her sister, who saw two words in big capital letters, **YOU'RE MEAN**.

"I can't say it anymore in this house, I guess, so we'll do it another way. We'll send it, too."

Ruthie knew the note was for Aunt Bea. She chewed her lip when Margie said, "we".

"Don't sign my name," Ruthie objected.

"Silly, I'm not signing any name. I'm just going to stick it into this envelope, seal it, put on a three cent stamp and take it to the post office myself."

The typed envelope read: Mrs. Bea Thornton

R. R. 3

Stearns, Minnesota

"Let her squirm when she sees that someone else knows that she's mean. She'll never guess it's us. That's the genius of it. It's typed. She can't find out."

Ruthie thought, "Should I tell Mom and Dad? Will Margie get mad at me?"

Margie noticed a wrinkle forming on Ruthie's brow. She didn't think her sister approved of the letter. She said, "Ruthie, if you believe in something, you have to stand up for it. Remember, you told me Sister Paula always says that if you believe in your religion, you must stand up for it."

Satisfied that she had convinced her younger sister, Margie went back to her homework and Ruthie fell asleep.

# CHAPTER 7
## *The Plum Tree*

Margie had chorus or glee club twice a week after classes. She worked on the school paper the other three days. Herman had started stocking shelves at Barner and Bob's General Store every afternoon except Wednesdays. With Mother working at the hatchery until four o'clock, the house was empty when Ruthie came home.

"There must be something exciting to do rather than sit in this lonely old house." Ruthie thought. Her mind shifted to what Margie said about standing up for things. As she sat alone at the kitchen table munching on a peanut butter sandwich, she heard a familiar whistle getting louder and louder. She saw Billy riding into the driveway on his bike, his feet on the handle bars and his hands waving in the air. She ran out the screen door allowing it to bang shut behind her. When he got to the steps, the bike tipped over right in front of Ruthie.

He said some bad words under his breath. Then he smiled looking for her reaction. She was shocked, yet admiring. Nobody in the Schmit family ever said anything like that. They had to say, "darn" if they became upset.

Suddenly, a girl from the public school on the corner, taking a short cut through the alley, grabbed a ripe purple plum from the tree by the garage. Classmates, imitating her, took plums while others started to stuff some into school bags. Instantly Ruthie knew that she had something to stand up for.

"Billy, they're taking our plums!" she shouted. "We have to stand up for our faith."

Billy giggled, "Why? Are the plums Catholic?"

"I don't know, but we are. And the kids stealing them probably aren't."

Billy, who was always ready for mischief, suddenly looked enlightened. "Turn it on when I give a signal," he whispered.

Ruthie caught on. Billy tiptoed behind the garage, dragging the hose. The lilac bushes provided a camouflage for him. Mr. Schmit had left the ladder standing by the back of the garage after he nailed down some loose shingles. Billy quickly climbed to the roof, pulling the hose as he went. He crawled to the side by the plum tree, signaled to Ruthie and SWISH. She heard squeals of surprise as the cold water hit the unsuspecting targets. They ran like hunted rabbits.

Ruthie yelled, "Puplicker!," even though Mother had told the children not to use that insulting name for the public school students.

Several drenched thieves screamed back, "Catlickers!" knowing that Ruthie and Billy were from the Catholic school.

"Puplickers," Ruthie hollered again, sticking out her tongue.

This went on until Thursday when Mother came home from the hatchery early.

"What are you doing? Turn off that hose immediately," she demanded.

"We're defending our faith, like Sister Paula told us," Ruthie said, but she couldn't fool Mother.

"Defending your faith? What does squirting water on some children have to do with defending your faith?" She paused for a moment and then asked, "What exactly did Sister Paula say?"

"You are Catholics and you must never deny that, even if someone tortures you and tries to force you to say that you don't believe in God."

"Were they torturing you and forcing you to say that you don't believe in God?"

"No," Ruthie squirmed.

Everyone, including Billy, had disappeared. Ruthie stood alone in the garden with her mother.

Mrs. Schmit said no more about the plum incident until after supper that evening. "Ruthie, tomorrow I want you to meet our new neighbor. She's Protestant. Maybe you can find a way to help her."

She knew what Mother meant because, when the Raynors moved in last month, Ruthie was stunned as she peered out her bedroom window. The movers in the big van unloaded the furniture, while Mr. Raynor helped his wife into a wheel chair. Mrs. Raynor had no legs. Mother had been over several times to visit the Raynors but Ruthie never went along.

The next day was Saturday. After breakfast Mother said, "Ruthie, are you ready to meet Mrs. Raynor?"

She nodded her head but not enthusiastically. They walked across the alley and rang the doorbell. As they waited Ruthie looked at the brick house. It seemed so elegant next to their own smaller wooden house with peeling white paint. This home would be big enough for her to have her own bedroom.

They heard some fumbling at the door. It opened slowly and a woman in a wheelchair said, "Oh, welcome, Margaret, please come in. And who is this?"

"Mrs. Raynor, this is Ruthie, my youngest daughter."

The new neighbor smiled and asked, "Do you want to race to the corner and back?"

Ruthie blushed, realizing that she had been staring at the place where Mrs. Raynor's legs had been amputated. Her woolen dress hung limply over the edge of the wheelchair.

Mrs. Raynor laughed at her own joke and said, "Let's go to the kitchen for some hot chocolate." With a strong tug on her wheelchair, she yanked it around and led them into the kitchen. As Mrs. Raynor poured the cocoa, she explained, "Two years ago I was in a train accident and the surgeon had to amputate both legs." Then, as if she had said something of little account like, "The weather is getting colder," she dropped the subject.

While Mrs. Raynor and Mother talked in the kitchen, Ruthie wandered into the next room with her cocoa, careful not to drip any on the varnished wooden floor. It looked like anybody's living room, until she saw a book on the coffee table by a lamp. Letters were etched in gold on the black leather cover, A BOOK OF LUTHERAN PRAYERS. Gingerly she edged toward it. Is it wrong for a Catholic to look into a Protestant prayer book? She couldn't remember Sister Paula saying anything about that.

She picked it up. Leafing through the book, she stopped here and there to read. She was disappointed that the words didn't seem to be that much different from those in her prayer book. She read, "Oh, God, Thou art my refuge and my strength," and "I will call upon the Lord at all times."

There must be something different, she thought, frantically turning pages. Mrs. Raynor's cough startled Ruthie. She saw the edge of the wheelchair at the living room door. She quickly slid the book back on the table as if it burnt her hands. Then she went back into the kitchen, hoping she hadn't been seen, or that her face didn't betray guilt. Mrs. Raynor showed no sign of irritation and when they were leaving, she invited them to come back.

At the door Mother abruptly turned around and said, "Oh, I almost forgot to mention, Ruthie and I would enjoy helping you with the mopping and dusting. Could we come at four thirty on Thursdays?"

"Yes, that would be so helpful to me. Thank you," Mrs. Raynor smiled.

"I like Mrs. Raynor," Ruthie admitted to Mother as they walked across the yard.

Mother smiled and put her arm around Ruthie's shoulder.

On Monday, Billy walked home with Ruthie after school. She told him about visiting Mrs. Raynor. "I got close enough to see where her legs had been cut off."

"What? You mean you actually saw where they were chopped off?"

"No, I saw her up close though. Her dress covered two bulges, then draped flat on the seat of her wheelchair." She then lowered her voice and said, "I read her prayer book, but I was disappointed."

"Why were you disappointed? Billy asked.

"Don't you see? Lutherans should be different. But her prayer book had some of the same prayers as ours."

"Do you think God cares?"

"I don't know, but I like Mrs. Raynor. She's nice."

Billy responded with a giggle, "Let's be *really nice* today."

"What do you mean?"

"Let's offer the plums to the kids when they come by and see what happens."

This time, when the children from the public school made a dash for the plum tree, they abruptly stopped. They saw Billy and Ruthie under the branches smiling at them.

"Do you want some plums?" Billy asked sweetly, holding out a fistful of ripe fruit.

"Here, take some. We've got too many. They're free," Ruthie coaxed with a mischievous smile.

No one took plums that day. And no one stole plums from the Schmit tree again.

# CHAPTER 8
## *The Revival Meeting*

Though Ruthie promised Mother she would respect other people's religion, the promise lasted only one week.

Margie came bursting into the house. "There's a commotion down the street and a huge tent pitched in the park across from the public school. It's a revival meeting," she said, shaking with excitement. "We've got to get Herman to help us fight the Protestants just this once."

There's that "we" again, Ruthie thought nervously. "But Mom said..."

Margie ignored Ruthie and continued, "I can hardly wait." She winked as though she and Ruthie were conspirators.

When Herman came home, Margie asked, "Did you see that big revival tent in the park?"

"I noticed a man, walking up and down the street, handing out leaflets," Herman said.

As they talked, a muffled voice filled the street. The children ran to the window. In the back of a rusted-out truck, a woman played *The Old Rugged Cross* on a pump organ. Next to her, a man dressed in a black suit, shouted over a megaphone, "All you good neighbors and God-fearing people, come to the tent tonight and be saved."

After dark all three Schmit children crept to the tent, hiding behind trees and lilac bushes, like detectives spying on gangsters in the movies. Then they let loose. Yelling and screaming, they stood in front of the tent. Suddenly, they were silenced by red flashing lights and a short shrill siren, as a police car came to a halt right next to them. Two policemen bolted out of the car and stood facing them.

Officer Mac McCarty flashed a light into their faces and said, "Be gosh, if it isn't the Schmit kids. Hey, you're disturbing the peace. Get in the car. We're taking you home."

Several of the worshipers had come out of the tent and stared as the police escorted the children to the patrol car. Shamefully the children slid into the back seat and the officer slammed the door shut. They drove half a block to the Schmit residence and announced their arrival with another short whine from the siren. The children, with heads down, slipped past their parents, who by now had met the officers on the porch. The adults were discussing the situation in subdued tones, while the three embarrassed disturbers of the peace, sat tensely on the couch in the parlor.

When the police left, both parents came into the parlor. Father said, "I'm ashamed of what you did tonight. What on earth were you thinking?"

Before any of them could answer they heard shuffling of feet and slamming of car doors. "The service is over," Mother said, "I want you three to come with me."

The guilty three followed their mother back to the revival tent.

Seeing the minister shaking hands with the last of the congregation, mother quickly strode toward him. "I think my children have something to say to you."

Herman began, "I'm sorry that I yelled and screamed in front of your tent."

Ruthie echoed Herman's words. Margie cleared her throat a few times and said hurriedly, "Me, too."

The minister, Reverend White, accepted the apologies, though he added, "Your behavior disturbed my preaching. You realize we all worship the same God. And many people came here tonight to pray. I don't think God likes all this fighting about religion."

On the way home, Mother said, "Let's take a walk around the block."

Nobody said anything for awhile. Mother spoke first, "I'm disappointed that you disrupted the service, but you apologized nicely and I liked that." It was quiet again. Ruthie sensed there was more to come because they passed right by their own house and started down the block a second time. Finally Mother said, "I wonder what your great-grandmothers would think about this?"

"I don't get it," Margie said. "They're both dead. Why do you wonder what they'd think?"

"One of my grandmothers was Jewish and the other was Lutheran," Mother replied. "Because Jewish ancestry is passed down through the mother's side of the family, that makes your grandmother, me and you girls, Jewish."

Ruthie's mouth dropped open.

"You have a lot of relatives who aren't Catholic," their mother added, "especially in Germany."

"If I'm Jewish," Ruthie wondered, "am I still Catholic? I know I'm not Lutheran so what am I?" She was confused. She knew her mother was still upset. She didn't want to ask her right now.

On the way to school the next day, she met Billy and told him about her great-grandmothers. "Now, I don't feel so bad that we can't fight the public school kids anymore because I don't even know if I'm all Catholic."

"We had a lot of fun with the plums, didn't we?"

Ruthie shrugged. "Everything is fun to Billy. He never worries," she thought. "What an easy life he must have. I worry about everything. Now I have to find out if I'm Catholic, Jewish or Lutheran."

She liked Sister Paula, but was a little intimidated because sometimes her teacher thought God was awfully strict. She decided to have Billy ask. "Billy, if a person's ancestors had a different religion than yours, would you still be Catholic?"

"I don't know."

"Would you ask Sister Paula for me?"

"Sure," he grinned.

As soon as religion class started, Billy raised his hand.

Sister Paula asked, "What is it, Billy?"

"Is everyone's soul the same or do the Protestant souls look different from the Catholics?"

Sister Paula paused a moment, inwardly searching for the best answer to give this young inquiring mind. "Every soul looks different because God makes everyone different. The important thing to remember is how we live our lives, regardless if we are Protestant or Catholic. Let me explain." She drew a picture of two eggs on the blackboard. "You know that our souls are not eggs and that we can not see our souls, but it will help me explain what I want to say. I'll color one egg yellow and in this other egg I'll make blotches." Sister Paula stabbed the second egg all over with loud sharp marks of green chalk.

"This," she said, pointing to the neat yellow egg, "is the soul of a person who is perfect. Someone with no sin. This other," she continued, pointing toward the egg with green marks and blotches, "is the soul of a sinner. We must always strive to be perfect like this one." She smiled lovingly at the yellow egg.

Ruthie envisioned her soul green and blotchy because of her hatred for Aunt Bea, and for not telling Mother and Dad about Margie's anonymous letter.

Billy poked Ruthie on the arm. In his desk across the aisle, he snickered, crossed his eyes and pretended to gag on the egg with the green blotches.

"God exacts justice and punishment for our misdeeds," Sister added looking straight at Billy, disappointed that this morning's new inquiring mind had slipped back into his regular antics.

Ruthie wondered, "How can he be silly about this, too?" But that's what she liked about him. He seemed carefree. She was serious about everything.

After religion they had art class. Ruthie knew that Billy was serious about that. He excelled at drawing birds that looked so real one would want to feed them. Their teacher asked the students to draw something about fall. Ruthie drew trees with red, yellow and orange leaves. She added a pumpkin patch. When she finished, Billy leaned over the aisle and studied the picture.

"Hey, that's goo-ood! Maybe you should sell pictures to help pay off the mortgage."

Ruthie looked at him puzzled. No one had ever praised her art work before. In fact, once Aunt Bea looked at a picture she made that Mother had framed. She said, "Did Ruthie *really* do that?" But it sounded more like, "Is Ruthie capable of drawing this well?"

With Billy it was different. She knew he liked her picture, because he added, "Maybe I could help you sell."

# CHAPTER 9

## *Aunt Bea Again*

Three sharp knocks at eight P.M. brought the Schmits to attention. Mom  put the sock she was darning back into the sewing basket. Margie, Herman and Ruthie looked up from their Monopoly game. Dad dropped his newspaper and opened the front door.

"Bea!  What's the matter?"

Shocked, Ruthie poked Margie and whispered frantically, "She's not supposed to be here until next Sunday."

Margie whispered back, "Listen, she's babbling about a change in the mortgage interest rates."

To Ruthie this sounded like bad news, especially when she heard Dad say, "Bea, come in.  What a surprise!"

Ruthie didn't stay in the parlor to listen any longer.  She ran upstairs before Mother could tell her to sit down and visit.  Though it was at least an hour before her bedtime, she put on her pajamas and jumped into bed.  "I can't stand to be with Aunt Bea.  Not in between times."

Ruthie didn't try to go to sleep.  She lay in bed imagining she was Lutheran like Mrs. Raynor.  She saw herself sitting in her living room by the lamp and praying from her Protestant prayer book, then answering the door bell, smiling and handing out cake and cocoa to the neighbor kids.

Ruthie put the covers down to her hips and pretended her legs were amputated. Then she edged her way across the bed on her rump. Finally she lay down again, closed her eyes, and imagined she was Jewish like Mr. Goldstein at the ice cream shop. She saw herself riding the sixty miles with Mr. Goldstein to worship at the synagogue in Minneapolis.

Outside, a car door slammed. Ruthie jumped up, turned off the light and carefully slid her finger along the side of the window shade. She lifted it ever so slightly and peeked out on the street. She saw that the headlights were on. She jerked back when she heard the loud *R-rrr* of the motor.

"I'm glad she's out of here. Her new car makes more noise than our old Whippet. How could anyone be so noisy and yet so boring?" she grumbled to herself as she dashed into bed again.

Someone trudged up the stairs. Ruthie's body tensed as she prepared herself for a scolding from Mom or Dad. "I'm sorry I didn't stay and visit," she would say before the correction could get out. Guilt was transformed into relief as the bedroom door opened. Margie came in and snapped on the light by the typewriter.

"Ruthie, can you believe it? Mother gave her a big piece of pumpkin pie and two pieces to take home for Uncle Don and Arnold. Then I said, 'Mother, shouldn't we save some for Dad's lunch box tomorrow?' And you know what Aunt Bea said? 'Margaret, I think you cut your children too much slack.' I hate that woman."

Ruthie agreed, but didn't say anything because Margie started typing. It must be another letter to Aunt Bea. She didn't want to ask Margie what she was typing because she didn't want to hear, "*We* have to stand up if we believe in something."

Ruthie pretended to be sleeping. An uneasiness crept over her. She lay awake a long time until sleep numbed her fears.

The next morning she saw an envelope in Margie's open school bag which she had dropped by the kitchen door. She hoped Mother would see it and ask Margie about it. But Mother was too busy getting breakfast for everyone and kissing each one as she handed them lunch buckets as they departed for the day.

Ruthie worried all morning about getting into trouble because of the unsigned letters. At recess she told Billy about Margie's letters to Aunt Bea. He said he thought writing letters without signing them was some kind of crime. He didn't exactly know for sure, but it scared Ruthie.

# CHAPTER 10
## *War Talk - December 5, 1941*

It was Friday evening. Dad sat in the rocker reading a letter. Herman and Ruthie heard a gasp from their father. Ruthie noticed his hands shaking as he read.

"What's the matter, Dad? Who is it from?" she asked.

"It's from my uncle in Germany. He writes that Hitler is a dictator and ordering the Germans to persecute the Jews."

Ruthie knew who Hitler was. The last time the children saw a movie, the newsreel showed soldiers saluting and yelling, "Heil, Hitler," at a man standing on a platform. Ruthie's eyes darkened with fear. "Mother said we have some Jewish relatives over there, and that Mom, Margie and I are Jewish. Will we be persecuted, too?"

Mr. Schmit looked sad and said, "No, I don't think they'll come over here, but my German relatives could be persecuting Mother's Jewish relatives. Or maybe they are hiding them from the Nazis. It's a dangerous situation."

Herman asked, "If the United States does go into the war, we'd be fighting Germans wouldn't we, like you did in World War I? Dad, your mother came from Germany, didn't she? Whose side was she on during that war?"

Dad didn't answer right away. He suddenly stood up and said,

"Follow me." The children were surprised when Dad climbed the stairs and opened the attic door. The attic steps creaked as the three ascended to the top.

"Why are we up here?" Herman asked.

"I want to show you something," Dad replied. He walked directly to the southwest corner of the attic. He knelt down, pulled out a cardboard box and opened the flaps. He carefully lifted out something.

"This is what I wore in World War I," he said as he reverently unrolled an olive uniform. Something dropped to the floor. It looked like a dead baby elephant's head.

Ruthie jumped back and gasped, "What is that?"

"This is the gas mask I wore."

Herman bent down to pick up the mask and studied it.

Father continued, "Your grandmother and grandfather couldn't understand why Uncle Jim and I had to fight against Germany. That was my parents' home country.

"Didn't Grandpa Schmit die when you left for war?" asked Herman.

"Yes, Herman. My father was so sad knowing both sons had to go to war. Four days after Jim and I boarded the ship for France, he died of a stroke. Your grandmother always thought that if Jim and I hadn't gotten orders to go overseas to fight, your Grandpa probably wouldn't have died so young. My mother dearly loved Germany."

"Why? Weren't they the enemy?" Ruthie asked.

"It was her home for fourteen years. After her mother died, her father brought the rest of the family over to America and came here to Stearns, Minnesota. Most of the people spoke German then. She wasn't happy to come to America because she missed her relatives and friends back in Germany. She didn't want to learn English. She wouldn't allow any of us to speak it at home. When I was six I went to a country school and had to learn and speak English. That was hard."

He stroked the army jacket. "I'm glad we're not living in Germany now. The Nazis are taking freedom away from the Jews and trying to conquer other nations. I wonder what President Roosevelt will do?"

The children stayed in the attic after Dad returned downstairs. Herman put the gas mask over his face. Two blue disks stared out of the goggled eyes at Ruthie. Herman looked like he had on an elephant's head because there was a wrinkled trunk attached for the nose. Ruthie didn't like seeing her brother that way. She distracted herself by trying on the oversized army jacket. Searching the pockets she found two sticks of gum.

"I dare you to chew it." Herman teased.

Ruthie took the dare and popped both pieces into her mouth. As she tried to chew, the gum crackled into little hard pieces. She couldn't make a soft wad anymore. She made a face and spit it out onto the attic floor. "Herman, how old is this gum, anyhow?"

"Let's see... 1941 minus 1918. It's twenty-three years old," he grinned.

They both started laughing uproariously until they forgot all about Hitler, war and persecution.

# CHAPTER 11
## *The Movies - December 6, 1941*

"Mom, can we go to the movies tomorrow?" Ruthie asked.

Because of the depression the Schmits hardly ever went to the movies, except for those starring Shirley Temple or Jane Withers. However, the theater manager had advertised two complete features and a serial for the Saturdays in December. Children under twelve years old paid one buffalo nickel.

Mother said, "Yes, I think I have an extra buffalo nickel in my purse. Would you like to take Billy, too?"

"Thanks, Mom," they both smiled because Billy was always so much fun.

On the way to the movie the next day, Ruthie, Herman and Billy dodged each others' snowballs. Finding this beneath her dignity, Margie quickly walked ahead of the noisy troop. Occasionally she looked around to see if any of her friends were watching such immature behavior.

Margie had bought her blue adult ticket. She was waiting at the door as the three rosy cheeked frolickers arrived at the ticket window. She could see Herman trying to shrink by bending his knees as he stepped to the ticket window. He silently placed a nickel on the counter. He had turned twelve last week but didn't have enough money for an adult fare. Without looking up, the lady automatically handed him a child's yellow ticket.

"If you don't have the money, ask me if you can borrow some. You cheated, Herman." Margie gave him a little shove.

When the serial began, a train was thundering toward a woman tied to the tracks. Even though Ruthie was sure the woman would be rescued, she crossed her fingers tightly. She held her breath until the masked man cut her free, just seconds before the engine came rumbling past.

The first feature kept their eyes riveted to the screen. Roy Rogers and Trigger safely got the gold miner out of a mine just before it exploded.

When the second movie was over, Margie wiped her eyes with her sleeve and sighed, "That was so good. We have to see it again."

That meant sitting through the serial and the first feature again. Finally, when Fred Astaire and Ginger Rogers danced toward the black and white sunset on the movie screen for the second time, everyone gathered their coats to leave.

Then Billy pleaded, "Let's just watch the serial one more time."

"Won't our parents worry about us?" Ruthie asked.

Margie hesitated, "Well, they know we're at the movies, so I guess we can stay."

They sat down once more in the soft red theater seats just as a uniformed man with a flashlight stopped at their row.

"Are you the Schmit kids? Somebody wants to see you in the lobby."

Ruthie saw her parents at the ticket counter. Her mother's face was white and her lips pinched into a thin line. Father's eyes looked angry, like the time mother said she was going to work at the hatchery.

"What are you still doing here? We drove all over town looking for you, because we couldn't believe you'd still be at the theater," Mother said.

"It's after seven  o'clock and you left the house at one thirty," Father added. "I was about to call the police."

Margie tried to ease the tension, "Mother, you told us that you used to watch movies for hours."

Mother moved closer to Dad. She didn't intend to get sidetracked from her sermon for the children. "We want you to promise never to frighten us like that again."

Billy stood uncomfortably behind Herman, trying to weave loose yarn back into his  torn gray scarf. The Schmit children felt chastened and there was no conversation as they  squeezed into the back seat of the Whippet. Herman couldn't stand the quiet any longer. Trying to win back his parents' approval, he asked, "Dad, do you remember what your uncle wrote about the war in Germany? We saw some of those things in the newsreel, *Time Marches On.* It was scary."

"Son, war is always sad and dangerous. I hope President Roosevelt won't get us involved."

# CHAPTER 12

*Sunday, December 7, 1941*

Billy's family didn't have a radio. Ruthie waited for him to join the Schmits on Sunday afternoon to listen to the football game. Just as the game began, Billy burst into the kitchen.

"Am I late?" he gasped, trying to catch his breath. He threw his jacket over the snowy boots he had left by the door. "Are you rooting for the Brooklyn Dodgers or the New York Giants?"

"Dodgers!" The family shouted in unison.

"I'm for the Giants," Billy exclaimed. He raised his arms in triumph and danced a little jig around the table. Ruthie, motioned for him to sit next to her.

At half time Mother said, "Let's make our sack lunches for tomorrow."

Dad cut Mom's homemade bread, Herman buttered it with peanut butter and gave the first piece to Billy to eat. Buttering another piece, he handed it to Ruthie who added jelly. Mom cut the sandwiches and wrapped them in waxed paper. Margie had packed her own lunch bag earlier and was reading upstairs.

"Shhhh, listen." Dad said as a radio announcer cut in.

"We interrupt this program to announce that the Japanese have bombed Pearl Harbor."

In the moments of stillness that followed this statement, the knife slid from Dad's grasp and clattered to the floor. Everyone jumped as if the kitchen itself had been shattered by the bomb. He picked up the knife. He clasped it so hard, his hand shook as he cut an uneven slice of bread.

Looking at the boys, Mother said, "Thank God, you boys are too young to go to war."

Panic and fear gripped Ruthie. Would they get bombed? Or captured? Would they be tortured defending their faith? Ruthie remembered the newsreel at the movies. *Time Marches On* showed Hitler standing on a platform before a crowd of people, all saluting and shouting, "Heil Hitler." Soldiers in smart uniforms goose-stepped down the street past him. She wondered if she'd have the courage not to salute Hitler, if the Germans took over the United States.

But Dad didn't talk about the Germans. Instead, he said, "I'll bet President Roosevelt will declare war on Japan tomorrow."

Ruthie was confused. She didn't know anything about a war with Japan.

Forgetting the rest of the football game, Billy ran home to tell his family. Ruthie ran upstairs, two steps at a time, to report the announcement to Margie. Her older sister looked scared, too. Hand in hand they went downstairs. Margie popped popcorn. Everybody sat around the table eating and listening to updates about the bombing.

A commentator said, "We expect President Roosevelt to declare war on Japan tomorrow." These were father's exact words earlier, Ruthie remembered.

Dad shook his head, "I wonder what this will mean for America," he said sadly.

\* \* \* \* \* \*

The President did declare war on Japan the next day. Father Weaver and the Sisters prepared a patriotic ceremony. An eighth grader carried the flag as everyone walked from school to church singing *God Bless America.*

One student from each grade read a prayer that Sister Loreen, the principal, had prepared. Her voice cracking and tears rolling down her cheeks, Sister Loreen said, "Our school stands for God and America." Father Weaver blessed the flag. An altar boy, dressed in a black cassock and white surplice, put it in a flag stand by the side of the altar.

\* \* \* \* \* \*

Within the week President Roosevelt also declared war on Germany. It seemed like the whole world was at war. The entire town seemed to be in an uproar as the days dragged toward Christmas. Unlike the sadness that her father felt, many people seemed excited and ready for revenge. At recess, classmates huddled in small groups telling about a brother, uncle, or even a parent who signed up to join the army, navy, or air force.

Though Ruthie feared what might happen to the United States, she wanted to read everything about the war. The Schmits couldn't afford the luxury of a daily newspaper.

One evening Herman brought home a used newspaper from Barner and Bob's General Store. "We can keep it," he explained. "Do you know why? Barner asked me to bring down a carton of canned pears from the attic today. I saw the daily paper on the steps and started reading about the bombing. When I looked up, I realized Mr. Barner was standing in front of me with a big scowl on his face. He was mad. He said he doesn't pay me to read on the job. But then he told me I could take the paper home after work because he reads it in the morning. Ruthie, we can have his papers free and find out everything that's going on about the war."

Every night Herman and Ruthie read Barner's paper and talked about the war. They looked at pictures of bombers, navy ships, and destroyed towns.

At first Father avoided any talk about the war. Then one evening after supper he walked slowly to the attic. When he returned he was carrying his World War I army jacket.

"Herman, please bring some nails and a hammer." Dad went to the front porch and, with Herman's help, stretched the jacket across the screen door by nailing the sleeves to each side of the door. Ruthie knew it was a symbol that Dad would support our country's efforts to bring freedom and justice to the suffering.

# CHAPTER 13
## *Christmas Preparations*

War talk diminished as the days edged closer to Christmas. It was replaced by thoughts of gifts, decorations, the Christmas tree and Santa coming to town.

Today was particularly exciting because Mother brought down the nativity set from the attic. Margie made a cave. She painted some sandpaper so that it looked like rocks. Then she crumpled the sandpaper around an old radio shell. It looked like a real cave. Herman took a roll of cotton from the medicine cabinet and tucked it around the base of the cave, so it would look like snow. They would wait for Father to add blue, gold, red and green electric lights after work. Ruthie tenderly placed the statues of Jesus, Mary and Joseph in the homemade dwelling. Even though the cardboard sheep she won in last Monday's spelling contest was somewhat oversized, she put it behind Baby Jesus.

Then Herman said, "Let's hurry with lunch so we can go to Gary's to get a bag of candy from Santa."

Ruthie had stopped believing in Santa Claus four years ago, when Billy informed her that the man in the red and white suit was actually Gary, the grocer. But each year they still went with Billy to the empty lot by the grocery store when "Santa" came to town.

As usual, Gary had decorated his pickup with butcher paper and, with Margie's help, painted the paper red to look like a sleigh. The bed of the truck held hundreds of sacks, each filled with hard candy.

Ruthie felt the electric energy of the moment. Parents and children were milling around the make-shift sleigh. When the church bell struck one o'clock, Gary, in his red and white outfit, hoisted himself into the sleigh and tossed the bags to the crowd. Billy, Herman and Ruthie scrambled to catch a sack, each managing to grab one before someone else snatched it. Billy immediately tore his open, looked at the contents and smiled. He jumped into the sleigh and whispered, "Thanks, Gary." Then he jumped out yelling, "Thank you, Santa! Merry Christmas!"

Ruthie noticed the unraveled gray threads of Billy's ragged scarf. She had an idea, "Why not give Billy the red scarf?"

At supper she said, "Dad, with your salary raise, and Mom working, could we afford to help Billy's family this Christmas?"

"That's a good idea, Ruthie, what do you think we could do?" asked Father.

She remembered last year when her folks had only twenty-five cents to spend on each member of the family. Yet, they enjoyed gifts that other people had given. Her parents had smiled when Herman opened a five pound box of chocolates from his godfather, Uncle Jim. Everyone enjoyed the Monopoly game from Aunt Bea. With Margie's box of chocolate covered cherries for singing in the choir, Herman's dollar for serving Mass and Mom's pink lamp from the school candy sale, they had a good Christmas last year in spite of their poverty.

"Let's pack a large box of candy, cookies, and nuts," Ruthie replied.

Mother added, "I know you don't have many toys, but why don't each of you pick out one favorite thing you own that you think Billy or his family would like."

Ruthie had only one toy she hadn't shown Billy. It was a drum and two drum sticks Herman and she had salvaged from the city dump. She knew Dad would not appreciate Billy's racket on the drum, so she never showed him the set. Besides, Ruthie cherished the drum set and didn't want to part with it. Instead, she thought of the magnets she and Herman had pulled from an old rusty car on Uncle Jim's farm. It was fun to pour iron filings on a paper and move them into designs by putting a magnet underneath. Relieved, she decided to put these in the Christmas box. Maybe Billy wouldn't recognize them. That way she could keep the drum set.

"Billy would have fun with these," she said, holding the magnets for Mother to see. "They're my favorites."

Mother said, "Yes, that would be a fun thing for Billy to have." Ruthie wondered if Mother knew she lied.

Ruthie blushed with guilt and quickly added, "Of course, we'll give Billy the red scarf that Arnold gave us at the candy sale."

"Excellent, Ruthie," Mother smiled, patting Ruthie on the shoulder. Both of them were unaware of the grief that scarf would cause.

Margie came into the kitchen and said, "Maybe Marie would like these blue barrettes. I haven't worn them yet."

"Great!" Ruthie said, "We've got two gifts for Billy, one for his oldest sister, Marie. We need something for seven year old Dan and eight month old Josie.

"I'll buy a set of blocks for Josie with my money from Gary's grocery." Margie said. "We need something for the parents," she added. "Mom, would you help me make some prune-filled rolls?"

"Why, yes, I'd like to do that," Mother agreed.

Herman ran out of the room, "I'll be right back, I've got something for Dan." he said. They heard some bumps and thumps coming from upstairs. Soon he appeared with a red truck Uncle Jim had made for him when he was six. Herman always treasured it and kept it safely hidden in the back of his closet. "I don't think Billy ever saw this." He laughed sheepishly, "I hid it whenever he came over because I was afraid it would get broken."

Dad said, "Tomorrow, when we cut our Christmas tree at Uncle Jim's, I'll ask if we can take an extra one for Billy's family." Then he added, "Come, Herman and Ruthie, help me get the colored lights around the nativity set while Mother and Margie start the rolls.

The next day the whole family drove to Uncle Jim's farm to cut two Christmas trees. "Let's sing Christmas carols," Ruthie suggested. Within a second the Whippet was filled with glorious harmony as the car jiggled over the dirt road to the farm.

After twenty minutes of searching in the woods, Herman hollered, "I found one." Everyone ran over to check out the tree.

Dad said, "The size is right."

Ruthie imagined the tree reaching to the ceiling in the parlor. "It will be the best tree we ever had."

Mother walked around the tree and scrutinized it, then said, "No significant bare spots. It will be perfect for hanging the ornaments."

Margie jumped up and down and clapped her hands to keep warm. "Hurry, Dad, it's cold out here."

"Stand back everyone," Dad warned as pine chips flew after each ax blow. A momentary sadness filled Ruthie as the helpless tree toppled to the ground, giving off its evergreen fragrance.

"Over here," Mother called. "This one is perfect for Billy's family."

Pine chips flew again and the second tree fell.

"Herman, let's put both trees next to each other. You grab the two top ends. I'll take the bottom ends," Dad said.

"Hey, it will be like lifting a stretcher, a pole in each hand," Herman said. They carried the trees to the car while Margie raced ahead, leaving Mother and Ruthie trailing behind.

By the time Mother and Ruthie arrived at the car, the trees were securely tied to the top. Dad cranked the 1929 engine a couple of times before it sparked into action. Ruthie, Herman and Margie huddled in the back seat, each wrapped in a woolen blanket. To distract the children from the cold, Dad started to sing *O Tannebaum* and everyone lustily joined in.

When they got home Dad pushed the Christmas tree into a pail of sand that Herman had prepared. Mother wrapped white tissue paper around the bottom to hide the sand bucket. She also brought down the box of Christmas ornaments and tinsel from the attic. As they decorated the tree, Margie turned on the radio. Christmas music filled the room. To Ruthie it seemed like heaven.

After supper Dad said, "Billy's tree is on the car. Let's go! Herman, can you carry that big box for the family?"

"Sure, mmmm, I can smell those prune-filled rolls," Herman said as he lifted the box.

"I'll take the Christmas ornaments," Ruthie said as she grabbed a smaller box that Mother had brought home from the store.

Herman and Ruthie sang *Jingle Bells* until Father parked the car behind some trees and bushes by Billy's house.

"Now we must be quiet. Ruthie, take the ornaments and open the porch door for Herman so he can put the box of candy, nuts, rolls and toys on the porch. Be as quiet as you can. I'll put the tree in that snow drift by the door. Then you two run back to the car as fast as you can. When you are inside, I'll knock on the door and hide behind that big oak."

With their plan of action in place, they proceeded as directed. Once inside the Whippet, Herman and Ruthie rolled down the frosted car windows a crack. They peeked out to see their father knock on the door. Smothering giggles, they watched him run like a deer toward the trees.

Maria, Billy's big sister, opened the door and saw the box. She shouted to someone inside, "No one's here. Oh-h-h, it's a big box --- and a Christmas tree!"

The rest Ruthie had to imagine. "Would Billy like the magnets or would he rather have had the drum set? Was Billy's father happy that someone gave the family gifts, or was he like Dad and didn't want help from anybody?" Of one thing she was sure. The red scarf was perfect for Billy.

# CHAPTER 14

## *Christmas*

Like every other Christmas Eve, Herman, Margie and Ruthie each claimed a corner of the parlor for their gifts. Herman wrote his name on a piece of paper and set it on the floor by the rocker. Margie put her name by the piano while Ruthie placed hers by the sofa.

"Is everyone ready to go for a ride and see the Christmas decorations around town?" asked Father.

"I guess I'll stay here and look for those extra Christmas lights in the basement," mother said, as usual, finding an excuse to stay home and put out the presents.

Though no one in the family believed in Santa Claus anymore, out of habit, Ruthie looked into the sky from the car window, searching for the sleigh from the North Pole.

After they looked at myriads of colored lights during the snowy ride, Dad pulled the car into the garage, knowing that mother would have things ready.

Ruthie thought that the depression must be over when she saw a pair of roller skates in her corner. A key to help her tighten them onto her shoes lay next to them. She suddenly remembered the mortgage and realized that the depression was not over yet. For a few seconds she felt guilty that she hadn't told her parents about Margie's nasty letters to Aunt Bea. "What if it was a crime and Margie went to prison," Ruthie thought, picturing her sister looking through bars at her, as she roller skated past the prison window.

"Look, I got an erector set!" Herman shouted, distracting Ruthie from her daydream. "I'm going to build a bridge!"

Then it was time to open the box from Aunt Bea. When Ruthie saw the books for her, it was hard to stay angry. How could Aunt Bea know how much she liked books? She was afraid to meet Margie's eyes knowing that, at this moment, she almost liked her aunt.

"Oh, no!" Mother gasped as she read Aunt Bea's note, "Listen to what Aunt Bea writes.

*Dear Jack, Margaret and children,*

*Arnold enlisted in the army last week. It is hard to see him leave us at this time of year. I'm grateful that Don is here with me, safe and healthy. We both wish you a Merry Christmas.*

*Yours truly,*

*Bea and Don*

This is terrible." Mother handed the letter to her husband.

Dad said, "Poor Bea. Arnold was like her right hand."

Herman stopped his bridge construction, his face pensive. Ruthie's and Margie's eyes met for a second. No sorry feeling here, they seemed to say.

At noon on Christmas Day, Aunt Bea and their own poverty were far from Ruthie's mind. "Mmmm, this smells good," Ruthie exclaimed as she sat down to eat sausage, sauerkraut and mashed potatoes. For dessert they munched on candy all day long. Mother had made small cloth bags out of white flour sacks for them. She embroidered their initials on the outside of the sacks. The master bag of candy and nuts sat under the Christmas tree.

Dad lounged in the rocker by the window. Mother read in the armchair, interrupted only when she refilled the emptied candy sacks.

Later in the afternoon, Ruthie could see that the sun was out and the sidewalk dry. She bundled up in snow pants and jacket, sat on the front steps, strapped the new skates to her school shoes and ventured onto the sidewalk.

Thump! She was on the ground. "This skating stuff is going to take practice," she said to herself. "It'd be more fun if Billy was here, even if we each had to use one skate."

She hadn't seen him since they left the box and the tree the night before Christmas Eve. She realized that she felt lonely. There was an emptiness now that Christmas was almost over.

The next day she got up early and grabbed her skates. She was about to put on her outdoor clothes when it began to sleet. Ruthie was disappointed. She wanted to practice on her skates but the sidewalks were icy. Instead, she helped Mother and Herman make apple pies in the kitchen.

About eleven o'clock Dad stuck his head into the kitchen, with a big grin on his face. "What are you doing home?" Mother asked, though her smile suggested she was expecting something.

"Look out the window," Dad laughed.

All three raced to the window and saw a pickup truck with a huge piano in the back. A man got out of the cab. It was Dad's boss, Ernie Anderson.

"Ernie wants to trade this for our old piano. Ernie's is a player piano with twenty-four rolls of music included. He wants to trade because he thinks the music sounds artificial."

Herman shouted, "What a Christmas surprise!"

After the men brought in the piano, Mother showed the children how it worked. She opened little doors above the keyboard. Inside was a box that contained something that looked like a rolling pin attached to both sides. Mother put a roll of paper that had tiny holes in it onto the rolling pin.

"These holes tell the piano what notes to play," Mother explained.

When she pumped the pedals, the keys went up and down by themselves and played, *The Little Brown Church in the Vale*.

"It's magic!" Herman gasped. "Billy will be here any minute and you two need to finish peeling those apples so I can bake the pies," mother smiled as she led them back to the kitchen. "Then the three of you can listen to all the rolls of music if you like."

Billy arrived breathless from his two block run. "Hey, what are we going to do today?"

"Wait 'til you see what Dad brought home this morning!" Ruthie said, prolonging the suspense by deliberately wiping the table and counters more slowly than usual.

"What is it?" Billy inquired, jumping up and down. "Hurry up and show me." Mother laughed as she put the two pies into the oven, "You three go into the parlor. Leave the door open so I can hear, too."

They raced into the parlor and listened to all twenty-four rolls. As Billy was leaving Ruthie noticed the magnets sticking out of his back pocket. She wondered why he didn't say anything about them. And why he wasn't wearing the red scarf.

# CHAPTER 15
## *More Troubles*

As the excitement of Christmas ended, war talk resumed. From the kitchen sink Ruthie could see Uncle Jim and her father in the parlor. She heard snatches of conversation, words like, *President Roosevelt, Europe, war and Japan.* When she finished scraping dishes, she sat on the stairs listening, Herman at her side.

"Do you think we were right to go to war?" Uncle Jim asked Dad.

"We both fought in the last war. We know what it's like. Remember, on Christmas Day, when we were in the trenches, we were close enough to the enemy that we Americans joined the Germans in singing *Stille Nacht?* For one day we shared peace. And the next day we went back to fighting again," Dad replied.

Ruthie noticed that Dad didn't answer Uncle Jim's question. Then she recalled something Herman had told her and blurted out, "Herman heard a customer at the general store tell Barner that things will look better for the economy, now that the United States is fighting."

Herman added, "Yes, the man said that war brings prosperity. I think that's true. We are not as poor as last year."

Mr. Schmit looked at his children with wide eyes. "Ruthie and Herman, you don't have to sit on the stairs. Come and join us."

Ruthie could hardly believe she was discussing politics with adults.

It was as if her life had turned a page and she was now grown up.

"It's terrible to kill people just to make more money," Dad said, turning to Herman and Ruthie. "What the man at Barner and Bob's General Store said could be true, but war is more complicated than that."

"Hitler is a madman. He wants people that aren't German, especially the Jews, to get out of the country." Uncle Jim added, "I think Hitler wants Germany to rule the world."

Ruthie was thinking, "If I lived in Germany, would Hitler know that I am Jewish?" She shuddered, "Would I be safe? I'm glad we live in the United States."

Father continued, "World War I caused a lot of destruction in Germany."

"Yes, and a lot of poverty, too. The people were ready for a new leader and a change in the economy," said Uncle Jim. "When Adolf Hitler came along, many Germans liked his ideas for reform."

Father flinched and didn't reply. He was proud of his service in World War I. He didn't want to think that World War I led to this war.

Uncle Jim went on, "Some of the German men who fought us in World War I are joining with Hitler, too. They want revenge for what we did to them."

The conversation went on and on until Ruthie felt sleepy. Mother came in and said, "It's time for bed."

During the night Ruthie and Margie were jarred awake by the

sound of loud banging.

"What's that?" Margie asked.

Both girls jumped out of bed and hurried out of the room. Mother heard them and was already at the bottom of the steps. "Girls, before you come downstairs, put on your shoes and stockings. Bring a blanket for your shoulders. It's cold and your father is trying to fix the furnace again."

Herman was already huddled on the sofa. Mother and the girls squeezed in beside him.

The next morning, heat from the furnace warmed the house again. Ruthie was still thinking about last night's conversation. She talked to Herman about it. "Herman, I'm so afraid that our German relatives might be harming our Jewish relatives."

"But you hate Aunt Bea and she's a relative. It isn't any different, is it?"

"It is different because we're not killing each other." But afterward she thought, "Is Herman right?"

Though the economy was better, the furnace got worse. The next night it stopped working again. It didn't even cough or chug at any hammer encouragements from Dad. It just stood there silently. The family lived and slept by the oil heater in the parlor for two days. Finally a new furnace was installed. When mother was presented with the bill, her forehead furrowed. Ruthie knew she was worried about the mortgage again.

# CHAPTER 16
## *Peg O'Toole*

Ruthie and Margie took down the Christmas decorations. Dad and Herman hauled the tree to the city dump after work. Now the house looked drab and Ruthie felt empty. The excitement of Christmas was over. When school started she didn't feel like going back but, of course, she did return.

She slowly kicked the snow off her boots before she entered the classroom. While Ruthie hung up her coat in the cloakroom, three of the girls from the north side of town were admiring each others' new Christmas clothes. Billy walked in. She noticed with satisfaction that he was wearing the red scarf. He took it off and began flicking it at one of the girls. Ruthie felt better and was ready for school.

At recess she walked over to the leafless oak tree by the south wall of the Church, where Billy and some of the other boys huddled against the cold. One of the sixth grade girls from the north side yelled in a singsong voice, "There goes Ruthie to meet her boyfriend."

Then the boys around Billy picked up the chant, "Billy's got a girlfriend." Herman heard it. He left the eighth grade boys who were making a snow fort. "Hey, Billy, want to come over and help us with the fort?" Billy dashed over to the fort.

During the afternoon recess Ruthie noticed that Billy joined the other boys quickly when he saw her headed toward him. He never looked her way again. Ruthie didn't know if it was because of the morning teasing or if Billy realized that it was the Schmits who left the Christmas box at the door. He must have recognized that the magnets and scarf were hers. "Not everyone wants charity," she thought. She remembered last year when her father brought home a box of used clothing from his boss, Ernie. Ruthie didn't want to wear any of the clothes to school in case somebody would recognize them.

When Mother came home from work that afternoon, Ruthie told her what happened at recess. Mother tried to help her sort it out, "It's probably the teasing, not the box. You're all growing older."

Ruthie couldn't understand why that would make a difference. She decided to watch her classmates the next couple of days. She noticed that the sixth grade boys were now joining the older ones in the 'No Girl' territory on the far side of the playground. Ruthie stayed with the other sixth grade girls playing *Pie*. They marched in the fresh snow making a large circle. Then they cut the pie into six pieces by walking from the circumference to the center, which was the safety zone. One girl chased the players, who ran around the circle and crisscrossed on the lines of pie pieces, until one of the girls was tagged. If someone was in the center or safety zone, the chased girl had to keep running. If she was tagged she then had to chase someone else. It was a favorite winter game and Ruthie enjoyed it wholeheartedly, but she missed playing with Billy at recess.

Now, after school, Billy stopped at the General Store to chat with Herman instead of walking home with her as he used to do. Though no one could replace Billy, Ruthie needed a new friend. Toward the end of January a new student joined the sixth grade.

Sister Paula introduced the new girl, "Boys and girls, you have a new classmate. Her name is Peg O'Toole."

Ruthie noticed a blush creep onto a freckled face with green eyes. She admired Peg's red curly hair. She immediately liked the new girl. She was pleased when Sister Paula asked her to show Peg where to hang her coat. The two girls would share Ruthie's books until an extra set arrived. This meant that whenever they read from their texts, Peg would sit on a chair in the aisle next to Ruthie, though she'd return to her own desk afterwards.

"Where do you live?" Ruthie whispered excitedly.

"Down by the city limits past the public school."

"I live over there, too. We can walk home together."

Ruthie thought, "Maybe this is the new friend I wanted."

The good news that week was Peg O'Toole but yet something nagged at Ruthie. Mortgage Sunday was in two days.

Sunday after lunch Billy and Herman were talking about sledding with cardboard boxes instead of listening to the radio. Ruthie felt uncomfortable, not knowing if she was invited to go along.

Then a knock at the kitchen door produced Aunt Bea. She wore a red hat with white imitation snowballs dangling from the rim. Seeing it, set Billy off on a prolonged giggle. Mother shooed the children into their coats and outdoors to play. Ruthie lingered on the bench by the kitchen door, fiddling with the snaps on her overshoes, deciding if she should go with the boys or not.

She overheard Aunt Bea say, "Why do you let them play with that ragamuffin? At least today he looks halfway decent with that old red scarf of Arnold's, instead of the rag he usually wears."

Ruthie held her breath waiting for her parents' response. She was disappointed when Dad immediately changed the subject by saying, "Bea, I'm sorry. I can't pay all of the mortgage this month. We had to get a new furnace."

Ruthie thought, " Why didn't Dad stand up for Billy? Why did I keep Arnold's scarf anyway? I should've thrown it back in his face."

Then came the worst. "Call me if you can't come up with the money, so I don't come over here for nothing," Aunt Bea snapped.

Ruthie couldn't believe what she was hearing. Everything around her turned black and all she could do was to focus on snapping her boots. She knew she wanted to get outside fast. How could her aunt say such a thing when the family worked so hard to earn money for the mortgage?

Margie appeared from nowhere, grabbed her coat and scarf and pulled Ruthie out the door with her.

"That woman is going to get a scathing note," Margie hissed through clenched teeth.

This time Ruthie didn't argue with her. They kept walking around the block until they heard a snort and a rumble and saw Aunt Bea's car disappear around the corner.

* * * * * *

Ruthie was getting used to the idea that Billy wanted to play with the boys instead of with her. Anyway, she and Peg were becoming good friends. On Saturday Ruthie invited Peg over to see the new piano. She didn't tell her it was a player piano because she wanted to play a trick. When she saw Peg come around to the back door, she raced to the piano, put *Five Foot Two* on the roller and closed the doors above the key board. Then she carefully placed a sheet of music over the small doors to make it look like she was actually reading the notes and playing. Pumping away at the pedals, she heard Mom in the kitchen say, "Hi, you must be Peg. Go through that door and you'll find Ruthie in the parlor."

Peg started saying, "Do you want..." She stopped abruptly when she saw Ruthie's fingers going up and down the keyboard and heard the beautiful music without a single mistake. Just then the sheet of music fell onto the piano bench. Without thinking, Ruthie took both hands off the keyboard. Because she kept pumping the pedals, the music kept playing. She picked up the sheet of music and replaced it on the rack.

"Hey, how do you do that? The music keeps going even when your hands aren't on the keys?" Peg's green eyes flashed anger. "Why did you fool me?" she scowled.

Right then Ruthie knew that Peg would be a different kind of friend, not like Billy who, by this time, would be laughing, giggling and trying to play the piano himself.

Mom called from the kitchen, "Girls, milk and cookies are on the table. I'm going to the store for some groceries. I'll be back in about fifteen minutes."

"Okay, Mom. Thanks. See you later."

As they ate oatmeal cookies, Peg told her something that made Ruthie sad. Three months before Peg was born, her father left and never came back. Her mother did housework for a rich lady. Unfortunately, the rich woman died.

"We moved here because there was a job at the hatchery."

"That's where my Mom works! What does she do there?" Ruthie excitedly asked.

"She candles eggs with several other women."

"I can't believe this. My Mom candles eggs, too. I bet they know each other."

When Mother came home, the girls ran to meet her at the door.

"Do you know Mrs. O'Toole?" Peg asked.

"Why, yes, she works with us at the hatchery. She's new in town," Mother answered. She looked at Peg and then smiled, "I bet you're related?"

Peg laughed, "She's my Mom."

"Well, I'm glad you're both in town. I hope you'll be happy here. Do you think your Mother would like some cookies for supper tonight?"

"Thank you. We'd love some! They're delicious!" Turning to Ruthie, Peg asked, now smiling, "Would you show me how you play that trick on your piano?"

"Sure, let's go in the parlor." Ruthie was glad that Peg wasn't angry anymore.

After explaining how the roller piano worked, she told Peg, "I really can play the piano a little bit." She sat down on the bench and played *Three Blind Mice.*

"How did you learn that?" Peg asked.

"My sister, Margie, plays the piano. Mom made her teach me. I didn't practice and Margie got mad. It's no fun taking piano lessons from your sister. She's a Junior in high school. Sometimes she thinks she knows everything."

"Do you fight a lot with her?"

"No, we get along, especially about Aunt Bea who collects our mortgage." Ruthie lowered her voice and continued, "Margie writes nasty letters to Aunt Bea and doesn't sign them. This month Dad couldn't pay all of the mortgage because we had to get a new furnace. Aunt Bea was real snotty to Dad. She said, 'Call me if you can't pay, so I don't come over for nothing.' Come over for nothing," Ruthie repeated, "like she isn't our aunt? Aunts come to visit, not just to collect money." Ruthie lowered her voice further until she was whispering, "I'm afraid Margie will go to jail if she gets caught. Billy said he thought it was against the law to send an unsigned letter to someone."

Peg nodded sympathetically. Ruthie smiled. It was fun sharing secrets again.

# CHAPTER 17
## *The Tragedy - March 1942*

Ruthie refused to enjoy Billy's giggling anymore. When he sputtered with glee in the quiet classroom during an arithmetic test, she pretended not to notice. When Billy went with Herman to the city dump to shoot rats without telling her, she acted as if she didn't care. At recess she flaunted her new best friend, Peg. The two of them walked in front of him whispering together. Ruthie pretended to be happy while her heart burned with hurt and anger.

Billy, like many people, was unpredictable. On a cold windy day in March when scattered snowflakes flew through the air and melted ice froze again, Billy approached Ruthie. She was waiting for Peg on the school steps. Billy wore the red scarf tied loosely around his neck. It looked pretty against the collar of his brown jacket. Ruthie decided not to mention the scarf in case he was upset about the Christmas box.

"Herman and I are going sliding down the big hill in the park. He gets out of work early today. We're going to use the cardboard box sleds. Wanna come along? My box is big enough for both of us."

Ruthie did want to go along....a lot, but she couldn't forgive so fast. Not after being ignored for two months.

"Not tonight. My best friend, Peg, and I have special plans," she snapped. She didn't say that the "special plan" was to study at the library, like they did every night after school.

The smile on Billy's face disappeared. His lips formed a thin line. He started to say something, then stopped and walked away. After a few seconds he turned around and said in his old carefree way, "Well, maybe some other time."

Billy went to the store and waited for Herman to finish sweeping the entryway with Barner's push broom.

"Hi, Billy, do you want a cookie before you head to the park?" Barner asked him.

The sugar cookie was crumbly and tasted stale, but Billy thanked Barner anyway after wiping his mouth with his sleeve.

"Come on, Herman. Let's get our boxes."

"Where's Ruthie?" Herman inquired. "You said you were going to ask her to come along."

Billy averted his eyes and said, "I asked her. She didn't want to." He hesitated, "The kids tease us," he added lamely.

At the park they saw that the big hill was snowcovered again after the late February melt. There was a grassy spot at the bottom where their boxes would come to a stop before they reached the road.

Climbing the snowy hill was difficult. Their feet wanted to slide backward. Billy reached the top first and jumped into his box. Covering his eyes with the red scarf, he tied it in the back.

"Hey, look at me. No eyes," he yelled at Herman.

"Pull that scarf down," Herman commanded.

But Billy didn't pay any attention. Whooping, Billy put his left arm over the side of the carton and gave it a push. Within seconds he reached the bottom of the hill. Horrified, Herman watched the box, with Billy in it, slide over the grassy area and fly into the street. At the same time he saw an oncoming car and screamed, "Stop!"

He heard the screech of car brakes. Then CRASH! BANG! THUD! Billy was hit. The red scarf launched onto a snowbank. The driver leaped from his car and knelt next to Billy's still form. He quickly removed his own jacket and tucked it around the unconscious boy. In the meantime, Herman, afraid to use his own carton, crept down the icy hill, digging his heels into the snow to keep from sliding. It was too slippery. Half way down he sat in the snow, sliding and braking with his feet until he got to the bottom.

Looking up, the man saw Herman approaching and yelled, "Go to that house on the corner and call the ambulance."

Herman bolted down the street, praying that Billy wasn't hurt badly.

Meanwhile Peg and Ruthie had begun the walk home from the library just four blocks from the park. "Billy is trying to make up. Billy is trying to make up," she thought. "He wanted me to go sledding with him." She would have danced down the street if it hadn't been for the icy spots.

As the two drew near the park, she glanced out of the corner of her eye toward the top of the hill, hoping Billy would see her and that Peg wouldn't notice her eagerness. But Billy and Herman weren't there. They must be at the bottom of the hill by the road.

Suddenly a nightmare of sirens shrieked, lights flashed and an ambulance squealed to an abrupt stop at the park sign. Then Ruthie saw the crumpled heap, covered with someone's jacket and a man hovering over it.

"Oh, God, please don't let it be Herman or Billy" she pleaded aloud.

As the girls dashed forward, Herman ran toward them, his face white, and his eyes black with fright.

"Billy got hit by a car," He said. "He slid down the hill and over the grass. His box kept going right into the street. I should have stopped him from putting that scarf over his eyes." Herman's voice cracked and tears rolled down his cheeks.

"What do you mean? His scarf over his eyes?" Ruthie screamed.

"Well, he was being silly."

"Why didn't you stop him?"

"I tried to... but Billy went down the hill before I could get close to him."

Peg turned quickly and shouted over her shoulder, "I'll get his mother." She was out of sight in seconds.

Ruthie stood helplessly watching the ambulance crew take Billy's pulse. Then she saw her own mother coming through the park, carrying a bag of groceries.

"Mom," she screamed running toward her, "Billy's hurt!"

Clinging to her mother's hand, she watched the crew carefully wrap Billy in blankets and strap him onto a stretcher. As they put him into the ambulance, Billy's mother came running with the baby in her arms. Mrs. Schmit put the groceries on the ground and reached out for the baby. "Alice, I'll take care of the children. You go with Billy."

"Thanks Margaret," she said as she rushed into the back of the ambulance. Through the window Ruthie saw her, sitting next to her unconscious son, stroking his forehead.

The sirens shrieked again and the small crowd that had gathered rushed away to tell their families about the accident.

"Herman and Ruthie, go home and tell your father that I am over at Billy's, taking care of the children. I'll come back when I can," Mother said.

Herman picked up the groceries. As if in a trance, Ruthie picked up Billy's red scarf from the snowbank and put it in her book bag. When she got home she took the library books and the scarf from the bag. She pulled her treasure box from under her bed. She would keep the scarf for Billy until he came home from the hospital. As she folded it she saw that two drops of blood had clung to the fringe. Smoothing the fringe between the folds, she placed it on top of her treasures, closed the box and put it back under the bed.

There was a hush in the house that evening. Mother came home at seven thirty. Taking off her coat she said, "Billy's Dad just got home from the hospital. Billy isn't doing well."

Herman's chin quivered. He said, "I was there. I told him to take the scarf off his eyes. But he kept right on going."

Ruthie's voice shook, "We shouldn't have given him that scarf."

Trying to comfort them, Dad said, "Don't blame yourselves. It was an accident."

Tears flowed down Ruthie's cheeks. She thought, "How could I snub Billy's invitation and refuse to make up?" She knew she would never tell anyone.

Mr. Schmit put his arms around Herman and Ruthie and assured them, "Ice is tricky. The accident was not your fault."

The next morning before class started, the students, gathering in quiet groups, whispered about the accident. When the bell rang everyone immediately went to their desks. Sister Paula led the opening prayer. She had tears in her eyes when she prayed, "God, you know that our friend, Billy, was in a bad accident last night. Please help him to quickly recover and come back to school soon. Amen."

Ruthie added her own prayer silently, "Please, God, help Billy. He is my best friend."

Religion class started. When it was Ruthie's turn to read from the Bible History book, she couldn't get the words out. She could only think of Billy in the hospital. Waiting for her to read, the children sat silently. The only sound they could hear was the ticking of the big round clock. A knock on the door made the whole class jump. Sister Paula opened the door. Father Weaver stood there and whispered something to her. Ruthie held her breath. "Is this about Billy?" she wondered.

Sister Paula slowly and quietly closed the door. Even before she spoke, her face told Ruthie what happened. "Boys and girls, I have sad news. Billy died this morning at eight fifteen when we were at Mass. May he rest in peace."

"Amen," the class answered automatically.

Sister Paula continued, "Father Weaver said we should close school for today."

Ruthie marched out of school with the others. But as soon as they reached the sidewalk she broke away and ran home, sobbing loudly.

# CHAPTER 18
## *Grieving*

Father Weaver prayed for Billy at Sunday Mass. He announced that the wake would be at three o'clock that afternoon and the funeral on Monday morning.

That afternoon Ruthie and the family went to Billy's house. Ruthie had seen one dead person before. That was when Mrs. Mueller, who donated a large amount of money to the church, died. Ruthie was in fourth grade. All the classes marched across the street to her house where she was laid out in her coffin. The students walked past her body in a single line, praying the rosary in unison. Ruthie remembered Billy bragging that he touched Mrs. Mueller's forehead and that it was really cold.

Now it was Billy's house where people stood in the yard talking softly. Inside, others whispered and sat on folding chairs placed against the parlor walls. Ruthie saw the casket at the farther end. A kneeler was in front of it.

While Mother and Father talked to Billy's parents, Ruthie edged over to the casket. She looked at Billy's face. It was so white. He had the same smile she had seen often after he played a trick on someone. She thought she saw him breathe. She looked again. No, it was her imagination. She touched his forehead. "It's cold. Hard," she thought.

Ruthie felt a hand on her shoulder. It was Dad. Herman and mother were on the kneeling bench. Herman was crying. Mother hugged him and gave him her handkerchief. Soon the people outside came in. They stood in the middle of the room because all of the chairs were filled. Father Weaver led the rosary. Ruthie couldn't pull her eyes away from the casket. Instead of praying with the others she kept thinking, "Nothing will be the same without Billy. He is my best friend. He *was* my best friend." With this last thought Ruthie sobbed out loud. Both Mom and Dad put their arms around her.

When Father Weaver finished the prayers, they left. It seemed as if the skies were crying, too, as they stepped out into the freezing drizzle. On the way home Ruthie's sadness turned to anger. "How could Billy be so foolish putting that red scarf over his eyes and then sliding down the hill," she wondered.

When they got home she couldn't eat supper and went upstairs to lie on her bed. Pictures of Billy and all the fun things they did kept floating through her mind. "Why didn't I say 'Yes' when he tried to make up?" Tears flowed until she thought she'd never stop crying. She fell asleep.

When she opened her eyes, the light was on. A peanut butter sandwich and a glass of milk had been placed on the table next to her side of the bed. Margie was asleep with her arm over Ruthie's waist.

\*   \*   \*   \*   \*   \*

When they arrived at the Church for the funeral, the ushers were throwing sand on the steps and sidewalk. Yesterday's drizzle had turned to ice. The Schmits sat right behind Billy's family. During the sermon Father Weaver said, "Now we have another saint in heaven. Billy is with God."

At these words Ruthie felt sweaty with shock. She remembered the time Billy squirted water on the Protestant kids stealing plums. Then there was the time he fell off his bike and said some bad words. She remembered Billy snickering and gagging over the boiled egg Sister Paula drew on the board and how her teacher's stern eyes looked straight at Billy as she said, "God exacts justice and punishment for our misdeeds." A horrible thought crept into her mind. "Was Billy really in heaven?"

Then tears streamed down her cheeks as she recalled how Billy praised her art work. She would tell God about all the good things Billy did. She prayed:

*Dear God,*

*Billy was a good boy. He was my best friend.*

*He complimented me on my art picture and*

*said he'd help me sell my pictures to help pay*

*the mortgage. He made us laugh a lot. Please*

*take Billy to heaven. Amen.*

After a pause she continued,

*Billy, let me know if you are in heaven. I've got*

*to know.*

When they came out of Church, following the casket, Ruthie gasped. The trees that lined both sides of the street glistened with ice. The sun was shining on the branches and the street looked like a canopy of Christmas lights. "I can almost see Billy dancing around those trees," she thought.

# CHAPTER 19
## *Ration Stamps - May 1942*

Two months after Billy died, the classroom still seemed empty and dull without him. Even though her father said it was an accident, Ruthie blamed herself for not going to the park with Billy. She'd get angry with him about the red scarf. But mostly she was sad because she couldn't tell Billy how sorry she was about not making up with him. Some nights she cried quietly under the covers while Margie did her homework. Sometimes she longed to open the treasure box and look at the scarf but she just couldn't make herself do it. It was hard to tell anyone how she felt. She had sworn to herself that she'd never tell anybody that she refused Billy's invitation before he died. She knew her father would say, "You shouldn't feel that way. It was an accident."

Mother had already told her, "Thank God you weren't along. You might have been in the cardboard box with Billy when it got hit by the car."

Peg never did like Billy because she thought he was a show-off. Ruthie didn't mention anything about it to her.

Margie always changed the subject. She had been preoccupied with her work since rationing started this month. She said, "It's complicated working at Gary's Grocery with those darn ration stamps."

Ruthie thought Herman understood her feelings but he wouldn't talk about the accident. Instead he spent more time with her. For the past two weeks they had been shopping for the groceries together because he didn't have to work on Wednesdays.

Mother explained about ration stamps. The war took a lot of the country's supplies. The government told the citizens to cut back on sugar, butter, cheese, meat and even some canned goods. To make it fair, each person was given a ration book.

This Wednesday Herman and Ruthie had finished the grocery shopping and were two customers away from the cashier, when Herman asked, "Ruthie, where is the sugar stamp I gave you when we came in? We need it to pay the lady."

Ruthie looked at her hand but the stamp was gone. "I don't know. Maybe I dropped it."

"We've gotten groceries from every single aisle," Herman sighed with a tiny edge of impatience.

"What are we going to do?" Ruthie felt a wave of hot prickles rush to her face and she couldn't look at Herman. She remembered Herman telling her not to bend or twist the coupon. Ruthie hadn't realize she was bending it back and forth until she saw a white line creased in the middle of the stamp.

"We'll have to look for it," Herman said. They retraced their steps. Then she remembered that Herman asked her to get two bottles of milk. The bottles were slippery and she had to use both hands.

"Maybe it's by the milk icebox," Ruthie whispered because she was afraid her voice would crack if she talked normally.

"Well, you go look then," Herman said sharply.

Ashamed and not wanting to take full blame, her quick mind silently accused Herman for asking her to get the milk in the first place. "So it really is his fault," she whispered.

After her thorough search by the milk section Herman said, "Well, we'll just have to buy the stuff we've got. It's late. Maybe the lady at the counter will let us have the sugar without a stamp."

His wishful tone relaxed his sister's guilt.

"Where is your ration stamp for the sugar?" the lady at the counter asked.

"She lost it." Hurriedly Herman added, "Mother gave us one but now it's gone."

"Maybe your mother has another one at home. We'll add these things up and when you get the other stamp, come back and you can have the sugar." Her eyes were kind but her mouth was firm. They went home not knowing what to expect from Mother.

"We don't have another sugar stamp," Mother said. "Ruthie and Herman, you need to go back to the store and look again."

The night was creeping onto the streets and a brisk wind tingled the tiny hairs on Ruthie's legs as they trudged back the three blocks to the grocery store. The bell over the door jingled and the lady at the cash register looked up but she didn't smile when she saw their glum faces.

"Mother said we have to look for it. She doesn't have another one," Herman explained.

They scrutinized every wooden floorboard but couldn't find the stamp. By now the store was almost empty of customers.

"Let's go around again," Herman sighed.

They were tired after the second round. The search ended right in front of the cashier who asked, "Did you find it?"

Holding back tears, Ruthie managed a squeaky, "No."

The lady reached under the counter and brought out a ration book. "Sometimes people give me their extra rations if they don't need them. Let's see if there is one for sugar in here," she said as she flipped through the book. "Here's one. You can have this one." She seemed as relieved as the two young customers standing before her. She reached for the bag of sugar.

Ruthie's mouth quivered but she managed a weak smile and said, "Thank you. Mother will be so happy."

Herman exclaimed, "WOW, THANK YOU, MA'AM! THANK YOU VERY MUCH!"

The blackened sky allowed the street lights to do their work. The children cast dark shadows on the storefronts as they raced home lightheartedly. The house was warm. They could smell Mom's favorite beef stew bubbling on the stove as soon as they entered the kitchen.

"I could eat a horse," Herman laughed as he put the sugar in the pantry. "Let's eat."

They all gathered in the kitchen washing hands, setting the table, putting the food into bowls and telling the story of the lost ration stamp.

"God, bless the kind lady at the store who gave Ruthie and Herman a ration stamp today. We thank you for the food before us. And we ask that the war will come to an end soon. Amen." Mother prayed.

"Amen," the family responded.

As they began eating, Dad asked mother, "Margaret, are we ready for the blackout?"

"Wha - wha- what do you mean?" Ruthie stuttered.

Mr. Schmit, recognizing her fear, explained, "Tomorrow we have to practice for air raids. Here in Minnesota the chance of getting bombed is remote. But the government wants us to be ready just in case. Everyone is asked to cover windows so light can't be seen by a pilot in an airplane. Each town needs to be in complete darkness."

The next day mother bought heavy black material and sewed curtains. When it got dark the family turned on a few lights. Ruthie joined her father outside to check if there were any slivers of light seeping through the blackout curtains. Not a light could be seen.

Other changes were happening, too. Some movies showed Japanese and German soldiers' brutality, unlike the U.S. soldiers who were shown as kind and brave. Mr. Schmit called these "propaganda movies." But Ruthie knew he believed in the United States. His army jacket on the front porch door proved his patriotism.

People in town began to put Blue Star Service Banners in their front windows. The small flags had a white rectangle with a blue star inside a bright red border. Wherever they went Ruthie and Peg counted the stars. A blue star meant that a family had a soldier in service. One day they saw a banner with a gold star. They knew that this home was sad because their serviceman was killed in action.

# CHAPTER 20
## *Aunt Bea Visits*

The phone rang twice. Mother answered it. She caught her breath and said, "Oh, no." After a long pause she said, "Yes, sure, okay. We'll see you tonight."

When Mother hung up the phone, Ruthie noticed that her rosy cheeks had faded. She looked serious. "Your Uncle Don is in the hospital. Aunt Bea thinks he had a stroke. The doctor says it will be awhile before he can go back home."

Ruthie felt a tinge of sadness for Aunt Bea. She didn't know Uncle Don well because he never came to collect the mortgage with Aunt Bea. If the Schmits went to visit them, he usually sat on the porch and smoked his pipe. He appeared to be a quiet man. He talked to Dad or didn't talk at all. She was almost positive Uncle Don didn't even know her name.

But she felt sad for Aunt Bea only for a fleeting moment because Mother added, "The hospital is within walking distance from our house. She doesn't drive and wants to stay here for two weeks."

Margie and Ruthie looked at each other. "Two weeks!" they both screamed at once. "She better not talk about the mortgage," Margie pouted.

Herman said, "Give her a break, Margie."

"Yes," Mother said firmly. "Aunt Bea is suffering right now. She is welcomed in this house. Father will go and get her tonight."

That evening as Ruthie and Margie brushed their teeth, they heard a car door slam. Quickly finishing their oral hygiene, the girls reached the kitchen just as Aunt Bea and Father came in. He carried a suitcase and a box. Aunt Bea wore an oversized brown felt hat that had slipped over her left eye. Ruthie supposed she couldn't straighten it because she had a paper sack in one arm and a purse almost as big in the other forewarning a long visit. Mother gave her sister-in-law a hug and grabbed the paper sack.

As Aunt Bea thanked Father, she plunked her purse on a chair and took the box from him. As if ridding herself of some unwanted burden, she dumped the contents onto the table. Books tumbled out.

"I love books," she choked and started to cry. Ruthie stared uncomfortably. She had seen her mother cry and even her Dad had tears at Billy's funeral. But Aunt Bea? It was nearly impossible to realize that Aunt Bea *could* cry. She watched her aunt take out a handkerchief with embroidered yellow flowers in the corners and loudly blow her nose. Pushing her hat back from her left eye, she set it rigidly in place on her head and patted it as if to say, "Stay there." She became herself again.

After she cleared her throat she said, "Don isn't any better. And just before I came here, I received a telegram saying that Arnold is a prisoner of war in Germany. I'm so afraid for him."

Even Ruthie could never have wished this on Arnold. "Poor Aunt Bea," she thought, "first Uncle Don's stroke and now Arnold."

Mother said, "I worry, too."

Dad went, "Tch, tch," and put his hand on Aunt Bea's arm.

Embarrassed with this display of affection, Aunt Bea tried to gain control. She changed the subject abruptly. Looking at both girls, she said, "Your mother says you like to read." She began separating the adult books from the children's books.

Ruthie's eyes scanned the titles: A CHILD'S GARDEN OF VERSES, TREASURE ISLAND, THE MAN WITHOUT A COUNTRY and many others.

"You can keep these. My boy is grown up." Then she sadly added, "He'll never read these again."

Ruthie wanted to brighten the situation. "Thank you, Aunt Bea. We love to read. This is like Christmas," she said cheerfully and spontaneously gave her aunt a hug.

It did break the somberness. Turning toward Mrs. Schmit, Aunt Bea again changed the topic without warning, "Now what can I do to help?" she said briskly, as her flimsy brown hat jiggled down to her right ear.

"Nothing. Come into the parlor and relax. You must be exhausted," Mother said. Putting her arm around Aunt Bea's shoulders, she ushered her into the next room. Mother continued, "I'm so sorry about Don's stroke, and now, Arnold, a prisoner of war. Sit here and tell us more about it."

As the adults visited, the girls went upstairs. Margie closed the bedroom door, frowned at Ruthie and hissed, "You actually hugged her. You don't mind the mortgage anymore? You don't mind that we're sleeping on cots behind a screen here in Herman's room? You don't care that Aunt Bea has a big bed all to herself? In our room?"

Tired from work, Herman had gone to bed early and was already snoring on the other side of the screen. Ruthie lowered her voice, "But think, Margie, how Mom would feel if Dad had a stroke and Herman was lost and maybe being tortured."

She snapped, "For Pete's sake, that doesn't change anything about the mortgage."

A long silence followed. Sometimes Margie was a puzzle to Ruthie.

In the following days Aunt Bea was harder to figure out, even more than her sister Margie. Ruthie could never determine her aunt's next move. Sometimes she'd have supper ready and the ironing done when mother came home. Then Ruthie would think it was all right to have Aunt Bea stay with them. At other times Ruthie was exasperated with her aunt, like the day Aunt Bea pursed her lips and shook her finger at Ruthie and Margie, because they argued about the color of the neighbor's cat, who was making frequent visits to Cinder lately. Dad told them, "Don't let the cat outside. She's in heat and ready to mate.

We can't afford any more mouths to feed."

On another day she tattled to Mr. Schmit about Herman and Ruthie having an imaginary boxing match in the kitchen with Margie refereeing. She told them, "If you've got so much energy, go scrub the parlor."

Ruthie had to admit her aunt never talked about the mortgage. Though the thought of another week with their visitor seemed endless, Ruthie lingered over Aunt Bea's books like she would savor a chocolate candy bar. Sometimes she thought her aunt was like herself when they both sat in the parlor and read books.

One morning before school, Mother took Ruthie aside and said, "Yesterday your aunt was told that Uncle Don will not get better. Will you keep her company after school because I'll be working?"

Dutifully, like a soldier, that afternoon Ruthie took her post in the parlor. She had gotten used to having Aunt Bea around but never had to visit alone with her before. They sat in the parlor, Aunt Bea in the rocker and Ruthie on a chair by the piano. Neither spoke for awhile. The grandfather clock ticked endlessly.

Finally Aunt Bea broke the quiet, "How was school today? What did you learn?"

What did she learn? Ruthie's mind searched frantically for an answer. She quickly thought of religion class. She recalled the day when Sister Paula drew an egg on the board and said it was the soul of a saint. She also remembered Billy pretending to gag on the egg with the green blotches, the sinner egg. She vividly recalled Sister Paula looking straight at him and saying, "God exacts justice and punishment for our misdeeds." Should she ask her aunt if that was why Billy died, for joking about their religion lesson and saying some very, very bad words? Was that God's justice? She had been worrying about this for a long time. She shifted her eyes to Aunt Bea, who was staring out the window.

"Aunt Bea, we learned about God today. Do you think God exacts justice and punishment for our misdeeds?"

Her aunt seemed startled and looked at her questioningly. As usual, she answered indirectly, "Arnold is a prisoner of war. Yesterday my husband was told he would never get well. Right now I'm wondering why God is doing this to *my* family."

Ruthie was shocked. Where was the answer she expected? The one she knew deep inside. "God is good. God loves you."

Unsatisfied with her aunt's response she told her more, all about Billy and his death, and that her own soul was probably not fit to be seen because she hated someone. Of course, she didn't say who it was. She told her aunt everything, except her refusal to go to the park with Billy the night of the accident. And, of course, she was too ashamed to confess her anger at Billy for putting the red scarf over his eyes. "It's terrible to be angry with a dead person, especially if he was your best friend," she thought.

Aunt Bea didn't change the subject. She didn't say that Billy died for this or that reason. She didn't say, "You shouldn't feel that way." She didn't say, "I'm glad you weren't in the box with him." She didn't even try to cheer up Ruthie. Aunt Bea listened until Ruthie finished her story. Then she got up from the rocker, walked over to Ruthie, stooped and gave her a kiss on the cheek.

At that moment Mother came home and they didn't get a chance to talk alone again.

# CHAPTER 21

## *The Letters*

Aunt Bea realized that her husband would not get better. Uncle Don would never go home again. He was transferred to a nursing home. Aunt Bea rented a furnished apartment on the second floor of a gray stucco house near Uncle Don. The first floor was occupied by the widow who owned the house. She gave Aunt Bea the key and the Schmit crew went up the squeaky wooden steps on the backside of the house. On opening the door they entered into a small living room. Freshly hung lace curtains and the smell of polished dark walnut furniture welcomed them. "Aunt Bea will be all right," Ruthie thought as she checked out the bathroom, bedroom and tiny kitchenette.

The next few days Ruthie missed her aunt. They had told each other how they felt about God. Margie would never understand.

After church on Sunday the family took Aunt Bea to her apartment. She invited them upstairs to enjoy some cinnamon rolls she had baked. Ruthie seemed right at home as she helped her aunt in the kitchen. Margie was furious because she could tell, without Ruthie saying anything, that she no longer had an ally in the war with Aunt Bea.

Aunt Bea seemed the same except she didn't talk as much. Now Ruthie would have welcomed her aunt's quick changes of topics. Two or three times she caught her aunt looking at her. Dad asked his sister if she would like to spend the afternoon with them looking for spring flowers in Uncle Jim's woods.

She answered, "No thanks, Jack. I appreciate your invitation but my back has been bothersome lately. I better stay here and rest."

During the following days Ruthie thought often of her aunt in the small apartment. The bustling busy woman now seemed lonely and discouraged. After all those years in their big house with Uncle Don and Arnold, she now had no one to live with her. Ruthie was angry at her Uncle Don for being so quiet. Her aunt had probably jumped from subject to subject just to get him to say something. Now he had deserted her completely.

She knew her anger was unfair, but she felt sad for her aunt and missed her. She decided to write her a letter. She told no one. She just wanted it to be like the visit they had in the parlor.

*Dear Aunt Bea,*

*I am very sorry that Arnold is a prisoner in Germany. I don't like war at all and I didn't like you when we worked so hard to pay the mortgage. I thought being relatives you should have given us the the money but I was wrong. I still hate the war and the debt, but I am very glad that you are my aunt. Father explained that you gave him the loan at a lower interest rate than he would have had to pay at the bank because he's your brother. But even without that, I'm very glad you're my aunt. Father says you have always been good*

*to our family. You don't deserve to have Arnold in prison and*

*Uncle Don sick. Our family prays everyday about that. The*

*depression is getting better and maybe the war will end soon.*

*Thank you for that talk we had last week.*

*Please write and let me know if you made any decisions about*

*God.*

*Love,*

*Ruthie*

*P.S. I have a friend. Her name is Peg. We talked about*

*visiting Uncle Don once a week during the summer. You*

*could have some time off. Since the nursing home is on*

*the back street from your apartment, would you like us to*

*stop in and see you, too?*

*The first two weeks in June I'm going to pick*

*strawberries to help pay the mortgage.*

A week later Ruthie was eating oatmeal. After breakfast she ran to the mail box and found two letters from Aunt Bea. One was for her, the other for her parents. She tore open her envelope and read:

*Dear Ruthie,*

*I am happy that you don't dislike me anymore. Maybe*

*it wasn't a good idea to lend money to relatives. But it*

*seemed a good idea at the time.*

*I have always loved you kids.*

*It's embarrassing to collect the mortgage money, but your Uncle Don always said, "They are your relatives. You collect the money." Maybe I seemed businesslike and you thought I didn't like you. Arnold was at the age where he thought and acted like he owned the world, which included your house.*

*I wrote to your parents and told them how much I appreciate their taking me in when Don first went to the hospital. You kids helped me keep my mind off my own troubles. I'm glad you like the books.*

*I am so sorry that your best friend, Billy, died. I wish I could help you feel better. If you want to talk about it, I'll be here.*

*It would be very helpful to me if you and your friend, Peg, visit Uncle Don each week this summer. Thank you. And please come to see me. I'll have milk and cookies.*

*Now about God. You told me your thoughts and I will tell you mine. After you asked me what I thought about God, the day we sat in the parlor, I thought about your question for a long time. Like you, I am Catholic and go to Mass every Sunday but I hadn't formed any conclusions about God. It was you, Ruthie, who helped*

*me come face to face with the fact that I was angry with*

*God. Why were these awful things happening, I*

*wondered? I started writing down my thoughts each day.*

*My thinking about God is getting clearer. Nothing in our*

*family has changed yet but I know that your Uncle Don*

*is in God's hands and so is Arnold.*

*I do know now, since you are so loving and forgiving,*

*God must be, too, because God made you.*

*Love,*

*Aunt Bea*

*P.S. I'll see you in a few weeks.*

# CHAPTER 22

## *Summer - 1942*

The day after school closed, Peg and Ruthie biked six blocks to the nursery on the north side of town. The sign, *STEARNS NURSERY,* had been freshly painted. The girls parked their bikes by several others, next to a large white framed house.

"Where do we get registered?" Peg asked.

Ruthie's eyes searched the gardens in back of the house. "Let's ask that man over there," she said, pointing to an adult in blue overalls and a straw hat. She was right. After they registered, he led the girls to the strawberry patch and gave each a wooden carton with six empty quart baskets inside. He assigned each girl a row to pick. They stooped down and began picking ripe red juicy berries. While filling her basket with strawberries, Ruthie became startled. For a moment she thought the blonde curly haired boy in the next row was Billy. Then she quickly remembered, "Billy is dead. It's got to be somebody else."

At noon, the foreman shouted, "Lunch time!" Everyone put their cartons down to mark the spot where they would begin picking again after the break. Stopping at the rusty pump at the side of the house, the two girls took turns splashing cold water on their sweaty hands and faces. They ran to get their sack lunches from their bikes and joined the others under the cool shade trees on the front lawn. Everyone was chattering.

Licking her fingers, Peg exclaimed, "These peanut butter and jelly sandwiches are scrumptious, Ruthie. Thanks for making them. I'll bring lunch tomorrow."

"Okay," Ruthie answered as she folded her lunch bag and handed it to her friend.

Out of the corner of her eye, she saw the boy, who looked like Billy, throw a football high into the air and catch it on the way down. Without thinking she hollered, "Billy!" Some of the children laughed. Others looked at her questioningly, especially Peg. Embarrassed, she whispered, "It's hard getting used to Billy being dead,"

"Let's get back to picking berries," Peg said. She never liked talking about Billy.

The time passed quickly as they each filled the six quart baskets. Ruthie enjoyed taking the carton to the foreman who punched a ticket with her name on it. She looked forward to the end of the day when she would get paid according to the number of punches on the ticket.

On the last picking day the foreman asked, "Does anyone want to hoe corn in July for fifteen cents a row?"

Ruthie and Peg said they could do it everyday except on Mondays, because that was the day they set aside to visit Uncle Don.

\* \* \* \* \* \*

On the following Monday the girls, flushed with nervous excitement, biked the one and a half miles from home to see Uncle

Don. The trip was tiring because they had to go up a hill. The nursing home stood at the very top as if guarding the entire town. A sign on the wrought iron gate read: ROYAL CARE NURSING HOME. They stared at the large red brick building as they sat on the long grass to rest.

Peg said, "Look, there are three stories. See those three rows of long windows with dark green shutters?"

"I wonder how old that building really is?" Ruthie asked.

"I don't know, but I don't want to be around here on Halloween. It's spooky," replied Peg.

"Well, let's go in. Aunt Bea comes and goes safely every day."

The gate creaked on its rusty hinges. A shadow of fright crossed Peg's freckled face. Walking up the long driveway, they saw a gray bearded man sitting on a lawn chair, a cane balanced across his knees. Using a large magnifying glass, he was reading a magazine. He never looked up as the young visitors walked by and presented nervous smiles to him.

They pushed against a huge oak door. Inside the girls seemed dwarfed by the immensity of the room with its high ceiling and tall windows. Ruthie looked around. She had never seen so many old people in one room before. Some were in wheelchairs, others in rockers or armchairs. A nurse, with a white cap, sat at a desk and motioned the girls to come forward.

"I'm Mrs. Linn," she announced. "Which one of you is Ruthie?"

"I am," Ruthie said as she stepped closer. "We're here to visit my Uncle Don."

"Yes, your aunt said that you and your friend were coming. Hi, Peg. Why don't you two stay here and I'll bring your uncle out to the lounge."

Mrs. Linn disappeared down the hall. After a few minutes she returned, pushing a wheelchair. Uncle Don seemed thinner and he didn't talk because of his stroke. Instead he squeezed Ruthie's hand and began to cry. It was a difficult visit because Ruthie had to think of all the things to say.

After awhile Mrs. Linn came over and said, "I understand that your uncle is a great farmer. He loves to look at our gardens. Would you like to take him outside in his wheelchair?"

Outside Uncle Don pointed to different flowers. Ruthie parked the wheelchair close enough for him to finger the blossoms. It didn't take the girls long to figure out that he liked roses. Peg ran ahead down the path to search for more. When she found a rose bush she'd flail her arms until Ruthie waved back, then point to the bush. When Ruthie nodded, Peg would race down the path to find more roses.

The sun was getting hot for Ruthie. She thought her uncle might get too warm so she parked the wheelchair under some apple trees. Peg joined them.

The summer breeze fanned them as Ruthie told her uncle about the money they earned picking strawberries and hoeing corn. She told him about Margie, Herman, Mom and Dad. Swallowing a lump in her throat, she decided not to tell him about Billy. It might upset him. When she looked up, Uncle Don was sleeping. Hoping not to wake him, Ruthie slowly released the wheelchair brake and carefully pushed him back into the lounge.

An assistant approached, "Hi, girls. Looks like your passenger needs a nap. I'll take him to his room. Thanks for pushing him in the garden. He loves the flowers."

Once outside, they could see the gray stucco house where Aunt Bea now lived. When they arrived at her apartment, she didn't ask anything about Uncle Don. She looked like she had been crying. Taking out her handkerchief she wiped her eyes and blew her nose. Peg mumbled something about going to the bathroom and rushed out of the kitchen leaving Ruthie alone with her aunt.

"What's the matter, Aunt Bea?"

"My life is different. I still haven't heard anything about Arnold. Nobody knows where he is and your Uncle Don can't talk at all anymore."

Ruthie felt like crying, too. Her aunt had a very heavy heart with Uncle Don's stroke and Arnold, a prisoner of war. Suddenly guilt hit Ruthie like an avalanche. "Margie's dumb letters must be a worry, too," she thought. She wanted to say, "Don't worry Aunt Bea, it's just Margie writing when she's in a nasty mood."

Instead she stood mute. Aunt Bea would hate them all if she knew the truth. Ruthie felt awkward, yet she took her aunt's hand and squeezed it. Peg, peeking in from the living room, decided it was safe to come back into the kitchen. Again, Aunt Bea startled Ruthie with her abruptness. She jumped up from the table, grabbed some cookies, placed them on the table and asked the girls about their visit with Uncle Don. Within seconds, all three were enjoying the delicious snack. Ruthie told her aunt about pushing Uncle Don in the wheelchair and looking at the gardens. Aunt Bea smiled.

"It's four-thirty. Maybe we should go," Peg said. "Thanks for the ginger cookies, Mrs. Thornton."

"They're really good, Aunt Bea. See you next week."

The next Monday dark clouds brought splashing rain against their faces as they biked to the nursing home. Ruthie balanced a pot of geraniums on the handlebars. They plodded through puddles of water and pushed the heavy oak door open at the ROYAL CARE NURSING HOME.

This time Mrs. Linn smiled like the lady in the *IPANA* toothpaste ad that Ruthie once saw in a *Life* magazine.

"Come," she invited, leading them to a huge dining room.

Ruthie sniffed. "I smell chocolate cake."

Daisies and carnations brightened the tables. Someone played an accordion. Others danced or tapped their feet to the rhythm. Those in wheelchairs clapped their hands.

"We're celebrating July birthdays," Mrs. Linn explained. "Your Uncle is sleeping now. Do you want to stay for some ice cream and cake?"

"Sure," both girls agreed.

After the party, Mrs. Linn said, "Ruthie, I see that you brought some flowers for your Uncle. Let's take them to his room. He might be awake now."

Ruthie picked up the geraniums and both girls followed the nurse. Even though the door was open, Mrs. Linn politely wrapped on the oak door frame. As they walked in, Ruthie saw that the small room was divided in half by a white curtain. She tried not to stare at the bald man in the bed by the door. His teeth were out and his mouth wide open as he slept. Ruthie wondered what it would be like to be so old.

When they approached the other side of the curtain, she recognized Uncle Don who was now awake. He looked at the geraniums and began to cry, but somehow Ruthie knew he liked them.

"Uncle Don, we've had a busy week since we saw you last. Peg and I have been farmers. We hoed the weeds that are growing in the corn field over at Stearns Nursery. It was a lot of fun and we get paid fifteen cents for every row we hoe."

"And the rows are really long," added Peg.

Uncle Don nodded his head and gave a little grunt. Ruthie knew that he understood what they were saying. "I'll have to tell Aunt Bea about this," she thought.

When the girls arrived at Aunt Bea's, they found her pacing the living room floor, praying the rosary. She greeted them warmly and led them into the kitchen. They were enjoying molasses cookies and milk when Ruthie recognized Margie's navy blue border stationery right on the table. She almost choked on the cookie. Her face reddened. She tried not to stare at the letter. She was quite sure Aunt Bea didn't know the letter came from anyone in the Schmit family. She almost blurted out, "The letters - they're from Margie," but she couldn't bear the thought of Aunt Bea's disappointment in her for keeping this secret. She wanted to hide under the table when Aunt Bea reached for the envelope and pulled out Margie's letter. She read aloud:

*You're a mean and miserly old lady.*

*I'm going to get you.*

*And you'll be sorry.*

Ruthie was shocked at the cruel threat. She knew she couldn't be silent any longer.

"Aunt Bea," she began. But her aunt cut in.

"I didn't want to tell you for fear you'd get upset, but I've been getting anonymous letters. It's frightening, especially now that I'm living by myself. Whoever's writing knows I've changed my address." Slowly Aunt Bea folded the letter and put it in her apron pocket. "I called the police this morning. This is a definite threat. I don't feel safe."

Ruthie moved out of her aunt's view. She felt sick. She remembered that Billy thought that it was some kind of a crime to send letters without signing them. "Now it looks like Margie will have to answer to the police," she thought. "I've got to talk to her tonight."

# CHAPTER 23

## *The Confrontation*

Ruthie's anger churned and she couldn't look at Margie during supper.

Herman was talkative. "Today was exciting at the store. Patrolman Mac McCarty stopped in. I overheard him telling Barner that he's working on a case. He asked him if he sold any parchment stationery with a navy blue border in the last few months."

Margie kept on eating nonchalantly, not even listening to Herman. Ruthie's last mouthful of chicken stuck half way between her throat and stomach.

Mom asked innocently, "What's he looking for?"

Ruthie was terrified at what Herman might say next. He said, "I don't know. It must be a secret case."

As soon as the dishes were finished, Ruthie followed Margie upstairs. She closed the bedroom door. When Margie settled at her desk, Ruthie stood firmly next to her and said sharply, "Margie!"

"What?" Margie asked startled.

"Aunt Bea is really scared."

A smile of satisfaction crossed Margie's face, "Good, that's what she deserves."

Ruthie's voice rose in frustration, "Did you hear what Herman said tonight at supper?"

"What?"

"Well, Aunt Bea said she called the police. That's why Patrolman McCarty asked about the stationery with the navy blue border."

Margie's smile disappeared, "You're making that up. There's nothing wrong with telling a person the truth about themselves." She started to breathe faster.

"Before Billy died, he told me it was a crime. You're going to go to jail."

Margie jumped up and clapped her hand over Ruthie's mouth. "Shhhh, not so loud. Ruthie, I was doing this for both of us. We're in trouble."

"I'm not. You wrote the letters."

"But you were in on the secret, so you are to blame, too."

Ruthie ignored her last remarks. She said firmly, "Margie, you have to stop this warfare."

Blotches of deep pink grew on Margie's cheeks. "What should we do now?"

"It's not *we*. It's *you*. If you write an apology to Aunt Bea and tell her you'll never do this again, I won't tell Mom and Dad. If you mention my name in the letter I'll talk to the police myself." Ruthie knew she was in command and continued, "Get rid of your stationery."

Margie was stunned at her little sister's demands. She grabbed the stationery and stuffed it into her book bag. "I'll throw this away at school tomorrow." She opened her top desk drawer and pulled out a piece of typing paper and began writing the apology.

Ruthie woke up several times that night thinking about Aunt Bea. She decided to go over first thing in the morning to tell Aunt Bea about the letters.

On the way over she silently rehearsed. "Aunt Bea, I wasn't the one who wrote those letters...No, that's not right," Ruthie thought as she pedaled her bike slower and slower. "If you promise not to get mad, I'll tell you who wrote those letters. No, that sounds stupid."

The nursing home was in sight. She knew she would have to gain speed if she wanted to get to the top. She remembered that Aunt Bea doesn't mince words. "I'll just say it when I get to the apartment." Puffing out loud she began climbing the steep hill.

She rang the apartment doorbell and Aunt Bea answered with a smile on her face. "Ruthie! Why are you here so early?"

Feeling stronger since she confronted Margie, Ruthie took charge of the situation. "Sit down, Aunt Bea, I want to talk to you."

Aunt Bea looked puzzled, backed over to the couch and sat down folding her hands on her lap. "What is it, Ruthie?"

"I had no idea they were threats. I'm sorry, I didn't tell you sooner."

"What?" Aunt Bea asked at this sudden burst of information tumbling from her young visitor. "What are you talking about?"

"The anonymous letters. They were from Margie. I know you'll hate me for not telling you sooner. I'm sorry, I'm really sorry." Ruthie didn't know what her aunt's response would be, but she hoped to hear, "That's all right."

Instead Aunt Bea said, "We all do things we regret. The important thing is that you told me now. There is something I regret, too, Ruthie, and I know you heard me say it."

"What's that?" Ruthie asked, surprised.

"I called Billy a ragamuffin."

Hearing Aunt Bea's confession, she decided to get rid of some more of her own guilt.

"The night of the accident I was angry with Billy and wouldn't go sliding with him. I've been too ashamed to tell anyone," she said sadly.

Her aunt took her hand, "How difficult that must be for you, Ruthie."

Feeling her aunt's support she continued, "I'm still angry at him. Why would he put that scarf over his eyes when he was going down the hill? Is it a bad thing to be angry with a dead person?"

"Oh, no," Aunt Bea said. "You're angry because you love him and you didn't want him to die." Her aunt, now feeling back in charge, abruptly got up from the couch. "Time for milk and cookies."

# CHAPTER 24
## *Looking for Answers*

Summer vacation was over. Ruthie and Peg knew they were more grown up. What challenges would seventh grade bring?

Sister Loreen was the seventh grade teacher and also the principal. Ruthie soon realized that her ideas about God were different from Sister Paula's. During the first religion class of the year, Sister Loreen said, "God loves you as if you are the only person in the whole world. People all over the world have different religious practices. Many religions call God by different names. But the main purpose is to worship God, the Maker of all."

Ruthie thought, "I like Sister Loreen. She helps me know that God loves my Catholic, Jewish, Lutheran person. If Billy was here he wouldn't gag, like last year, when he saw the eggs drawn on the blackboard. He 'd say, 'I like that,' just as he said about my art work. He wouldn't even giggle."

Ruthie was ninety-nine percent sure that Billy was in heaven, but she wanted someone official, someone who knew Billy's shenanigans, to say it. Sister Loreen was the official person to ask.

But first she tested Sister Loreen. "What do our souls look like, Sister?" If she drew eggs on the board, Ruthie would not ask her question.

"Your soul is invisible. It is the part of you that gives you life and spirit. It stays alive even when you die."

Ruthie thought about it. Then she said, "I have another question. Sister Paula told us that God exacts punishment and justice for our misdeeds. Is that why Billy died last March, after saying a bad word and making fun of what Sister drew on the board?" There it was, out before the entire class.

Sister Loreen swallowed hard and looked at her. "Of course not, Ruthie. Nobody knows why one person dies young and another lives past eighty or ninety. Billy's in heaven. He has a beautiful spirit. Sister Paula said he had a gift to make people laugh."

Ruthie knew she would never forget Sister Loreen, who had finally given her an official answer.

\* \* \* \* \* \*

School was going well for Ruthie and Peg. One day in October, the students were asked to help with the war effort.

"Boys and girls, the government needs some supplies for the soldiers. We are not going to have school today," Sister Loreen announced.

Some of the seventh graders sat in shocked silence and others whooped "Hurrah!"

Sister continued, "We want you to bring old newspapers, scraps of metal and rubber from home and your neighborhood. We've constructed an indoor slide by a window in the basement. Bring your supplies to the alley window and someone will help you unload. Sister Mary and I will record and the other sisters will bundle."

A day off! Ruthie was elated and proud to collect for her country. Sister Loreen smiled as the class trooped out of the door.

"Oh, Ruthie and Peg, I've got something special for you two to do. Both of you are good in arithmetic. I could really use your help to weigh the materials the students bring. Ruthie, you may weigh this morning and Peg this afternoon."

Ruthie wished her marks had been a little lower because she would rather have the whole day free to collect the supplies like the others.

"Oh well," she said as she replaced her coat in the cloak room and helped Sister Loreen take twine, scissors, paper and pencils to the basement. In all of her seven years at St. Joseph School she had never been to the basement. It seemed spooky as Sister opened a squeaky door. She snapped on the light and Ruthie saw the homemade slide. It consisted of three long planks with a linoleum strip nailed over the boards.

"How do you like it?" Sister asked proudly, "We found some old kitchen linoleum in the convent attic and thought it would make the slide slippery."

"WOW," Ruthie exclaimed. "Who nailed the linoleum onto the boards?" It was hard for her to imagine the sisters as carpenters or even pounding anything with a hammer.

"Sister Mary hammered and I sawed the planks. Ruthie, grab hold, please. Help me move this table closer to the scale. Now this is how we'll operate. When the supplies come down the chute, you will weigh them and I'll record the name of the student and the weight of what was brought in: paper, rubber or metal scraps. Sister Mary will help me record. The other sisters will separate and bundle."

Twenty minutes later, they heard the first shouts of young people returning. "Here they come!" laughed Sister Mary excitedly. After the first load of newspapers hit the slide, Ruthie was so busy weighing, she didn't notice the time slip by.

"It's eleven thirty. Let's take a break. Ruthie, you worked so hard. Thank you. I like working with you. Now this afternoon, see what you can collect and Peg will do the weighing."

"Mom, I'm going to collect supplies this afternoon," Ruthie told her mother. She proudly reviewed her morning's work and Sister Loreen's compliment. Ruthie knew her Mother was happy, too, because her eyes shone as she set a bowl of hot tomato soup in front of her and pushed a strand of hair off her daughter's sweaty forehead.

"Herman took all of the papers this morning, though," Mother said. She must have seen Ruthie's disappointment because she added, "Maybe Herman didn't know you were helping Sister Loreen only in the morning. Wait! I think there are some old rusty tools in the garage that Dad doesn't use anymore. When you're finished eating, let's go out and check."

After ten minutes of rummaging around in both the front and back garage, they had found one old black rubber boot, a large barn pulley, an old garbage can with the bottom rusted out, a split garden hose, and a bike tire that couldn't be fixed. Mother helped Ruthie arrange the supplies in an old red wagon no one had played with for years.

"Mom, do you think I could contribute this wagon?"

"Sounds like a good idea, Ruthie. The garage hasn't been cleaned since your candy sale. I think I can find another load of materials. Maybe you better bring the wagon back before you leave it at school."

"Okay, Mom. See you later."

The early October snow had melted, except for a few splotches on the city park. Ruthie decided to take a short cut over the soggy park lawn. She wanted to hurry to get the second load before school closed.

As she came over a little hill, she saw a large puddle stretched in front of her path. She decided, "I'm not going to lug this wagon back to the sidewalk. It's a block away. I've got boots on and I'll just walk through it, like I did when I was a little kid."

It was fun sloshing through the puddle. Suddenly, she found herself sitting in the middle of the pond, drenched. Quickly she looked around to see if anyone was watching. "Thank heavens nobody is looking," she thought. Ruthie tried to get up but her foot slipped on the floor of ice under the water and she gave herself another shivering bath. She remembered Dad saying, "Ice is tricky. Anybody can make a mistake."

Carefully she stood up and gingerly slid her feet along the bottom of the pond so she wouldn't lose her balance again. "The supplies are dry but I'm a mess. How embarrassing," she muttered. Chunks of ice clung to her snow pants and jacket. She felt like a baby with wet diapers.

Her thoughts jumped around for solutions. "Should I leave this stuff and go home? The time is going fast. No, better get to school. So what if the kids laugh at me. I can handle the teasing. Yuck, this is cold. One more block and I'll be there."

Later, Mother said, "You were brave to go to school the way you look. Ruthie, I can see what a courageous person you are. I hope you don't get a cold, though. Change your clothes. I'll make some hot cocoa. Dad came home early to help collect supplies. He is loading the Whippet with the things found in the garage. All three of us can take the supplies to school. If we hurry we can make it before the Sisters lock up the building."

By the time Ruthie got outside, Dad had hitched a cart to the back of the car and loaded odd looking pieces of iron and rubber. She didn't know what most of it was. Dad tied some rope around the entire load so it wouldn't fall out.

"Get in, Ruthie, I'm glad you and your Mother started cleaning the shed. We found a lot more junk that can be used," Dad said smiling.

"Wait 'til Sister Loreen sees this," Ruthie shouted and jumped into the Whippet.

Ruthie was exhausted that night. She fell asleep early and for the first time since his death, she dreamed of Billy. High on a cloud he sat on his bike, feet on the handlebars, the red scarf tied over his eyes. He started down the cloud, then pulled off the scarf. He turned to Ruthie and smiled a most beautiful smile. She tried to reach out and touch his face. When he reached the bottom of the cloud, he bumped right into another cloud. The bike tipped.

In her dream he looked at her again, smiled, and said, "Bye, Ruthie. God and I are going to play with the magnets again today."

"You can have the drum set, too," she was telling him as she woke up. Her throat was fiery and she felt like she had the chills. Shivering, she tucked the covers tighter around her. She couldn't get back to sleep again. She kept thinking of her fall in the water while crossing the park. She didn't realize it would be icy there.

Then, as sure as if Billy was telling the story, she pictured the accident. *Billy didn't keep the scarf over his eyes all the way down the hill. Billy was a comedian and sometimes a showoff, but he wasn't stupid.* In her mind, she watched him start down the hill, pull off the scarf after he was out of Herman's sight, then brace himself for a quick stop when the box hit the grass where the snow had melted. *Billy never realized that the grass was icy. The box kept going right into the road and into the path of the blue car.*

At breakfast she told Herman her theory. "Billy pulled off the scarf before he hit the bottom of the hill. Nobody could change what happened, not you, or me, or Billy. Nobody could stop that box from sliding into the road."

Herman's face relaxed and the tears flowed.

# CHAPTER 25
## *Healing*

Ruthie's throat got worse and her temperature stayed at one hundred two degrees for three days. Mother rubbed her chest with Vicks and warmed cloths on the kitchen stove to put on her chest. It seemed to break her cough. Because it was cold in their bedrooms, Father and Herman carried the mattresses, sheets and blankets down from upstairs. Ruthie, Herman and Margie slept in the parlor. The new furnace forced warm air through the grate in the parlor floor. Ruthie was comforted, knowing her parents' bedroom was right on the other side of the wall. Her body began to heal and she hardly coughed anymore. But sadness still weighed on her heart because she had refused to make up with Billy before he died.

It was a Saturday morning when the girls biked to the Royal Care Nursing Home. A late October Indian Summer had settled in. The sun soaked warm into their skin, though the leaves were mostly gone from the trees.

It seemed that Uncle Don slept most of the day now, but he was awake when Ruthie entered the room. She wondered if he still knew her. She asked him if he would like to go outside in the sun and crunch leaves with his wheelchair. He squeezed her hand lightly. She was reassured.

After several circles around the gardens, he began yawning. Ruthie took him back to his room. She noticed the drooping wilted geranium on the windowsill. Peg must have noticed it, too, because she said to Ruthie, "The geranium is dead."

"The geranium isn't dead, Peg. It just looks dead but there's life inside. I read about geraniums for a science report last year. I'll take the plant to Aunt Bea. I've seen how she pinches off the leaves, cuts the stems back a bit and waters these things. She is good with plants. Then next spring it will bloom again."

Peg had to go home early, so Ruthie biked over to Aunt Bea's alone. Her aunt seemed happy and busy, rolling out dough for Halloween treats. She was surprised to see her niece on a Saturday morning. "You look like you are feeling much better, Ruthie."

"Yes, I am. Can you save Uncle Don's geranium, Aunt Bea? It looks dead but I know there is some life in it still." This time Ruthie abruptly changed the subject. "Aunt Bea, I had a dream about Billy. He said he was going to play magnets with God. He seemed so real. Do you think Billy knows that I'm sorry that I didn't make up with him?"

"What do you think, Ruthie?" asked Aunt Bea.

Ruthie fingered the geranium. "How can this plant come to life again? But it will." Then the realization came over her. "Aunt Bea, Billy is like this geranium. Just because his body is dead, it doesn't mean that his life is ended. He lives and he knows."

That evening, for the first time since the accident, Ruthie pulled her treasure box from under the bed. It had a layer of dust on it. With a damp washcloth she wiped the box clean.

Ruthie carefully removed the lid of the box and unfolded the red scarf. The ache in her heart was gone. She felt only tenderness as she touched the two blood drops, which had long ago dried into dark brown spots on the beautiful red scarf. Then she refolded the scarf and gently placed it back into the box.

# *Epilogue*

Margie joined the Women's Army Corps after graduation and served until the war finally ended in 1945. Always seeking to right injustice, she became a lawyer and spent her life bringing justice through virtuous and legal means.

Herman continued his interest in business. Eventually Barner and Bob's General Store became Schmit's Grocery, expanding to cover half the city block.

Mrs. Schmit had long ago stopped working at the hatchery. She became the bookkeeper for Herman's business. She and Mr. Schmit continued to guide their children wisely.

Mr. Schmit was proud that even during the great depression, he was able to support his family, rather than go on welfare. He continued to show loyalty to his country by wearing his American Legion cap to all patriotic events.

Uncle Don died three months before Arnold was released from the German prison camp in 1945. When Arnold returned home Aunt Bea lived with him on the farm.

Though Ruthie kept the red scarf in her treasure box as a tender memorial to her friend, Billy, the pain in her heart did not return. She replaced it with peace and lightness.

As the years passed, her life continued to unfold. She decided to study nursing. After serving two years in the Korean War, she worked with the homebound, spending countless hours with her aging Aunt Bea.

Ruthie married and had three children. She named the oldest child Billy.

# About the Authors

Ms. Eileen Drilling, M.S. has written materials published by the Hazelden Foundation in Center City, Minnesota. She has also written short stories, journals and family activities for a series published by Liturgy Training Publications, Chicago, Illinois. She lives in Anoka, Minnesota.

Ms. Judith Rothfork, M.A. has co-authored the same series with Ms. Drilling. In the past, Ms. Rothfork has been a teacher, counselor and free lance speaker on spirituality and mental health issues. She currently lives in Anoka, Minnesota.